Pretty Freekin Scary™

~ Me So Pretty! ~

Grosset & Dunlap

a novel by
Chris P. Flesh

Continued thanks to Nancy Holder who
helped bring this story to life.

GROSSET & DUNLAP
Published by the Penguin Group
Penguin Group (USA) Inc., 375 Hudson Street, New York, New York 10014, USA
Penguin Group (Canada), 90 Eglinton Avenue East, Suite 700, Toronto, Ontario M4P 2Y3,
Canada (a division of Pearson Penguin Canada Inc.)
Penguin Books Ltd., 80 Strand, London WC2R 0RL, England
Penguin Group Ireland, 25 St. Stephen's Green, Dublin 2, Ireland
(a division of Penguin Books Ltd.)
Penguin Group (Australia), 250 Camberwell Road, Camberwell, Victoria 3124, Australia
(a division of Pearson Australia Group Pty. Ltd.)
Penguin Books India Pvt. Ltd., 11 Community Centre,
Panchsheel Park, New Delhi—110 017, India
Penguin Group (NZ), 67 Apollo Drive, Rosedale, North Shore 0745, Auckland, New Zealand
(a division of Pearson New Zealand Ltd.)
Penguin Books (South Africa) (Pty.) Ltd., 24 Sturdee Avenue,
Rosebank, Johannesburg 2196, South Africa

Penguin Books Ltd., Registered Offices: 80 Strand, London WC2R 0RL, England

Pretty Freekin Scary™ and related trademarks © 2007 AGC, Inc. Used under license by
Penguin Young Readers Group. All rights reserved. Published by Grosset & Dunlap, a division
of Penguin Young Readers Group, 345 Hudson Street, New York, New York 10014. GROSSET
& DUNLAP is a trademark of Penguin Group (USA) Inc. Printed in the U.S.A.

Library of Congress Cataloging-in-Publication Data is available.

ISBN 978-0-448-44683-7   10 9 8 7 6 5 4 3 2 1

Prologue:
In Which I Fill You In

* * * *

Welcome, Gentle Reader, to this book. I am Your Humble Yet Rather Nerve-Racked Narrator. You see, for years, I told thrilling stories of adventure, chills, and thrills about some extremely impressive VIPs—Very Interesting Persons. Humanitarians. Artists. Captains of industry. I did an excellent job, and all was well. I was happy.

But alas, one of my narrative subjects complained about me, informing the International Order of Narrators that I was getting underfoot and asking too many questions. I ask you, how can a narrator ask too many questions? Isn't that the job of a good narrator? To dig deep and get to the heart of things? Don't you think that accusation is simply ridiculous? However, ION sided with the subject, and as a result, I was booted out of my beloved organization and told never to narrate a story again.

I was in total despair. I had no idea what to do with myself, no notion of how to go on.

And then I came across the story of another person who got in deep trouble for asking questions . . . and, in *his* case, was given a second chance. I speak, of course, of Franklin Ripp, who died last June thirteenth, in a manner so completely and utterly humiliating that I have sworn never to reveal it. (Trust me, you do not want to know.) In return for my silence, Franklin agreed to let me narrate the story of his life. And it is my hope that if I do a good job (and why would I not?), ION will welcome me back with open arms, an apology, and perhaps a nice party with tea and cakes.

If, at the end of this stirring tale of thrills, chills, and, unfortunately, quite a bit of despair, you agree that I have proven my worth as a Narrator, I implore you to contact ION and tell them so. My attempts to speak with them have all met with silence, and it is my fear that they have written me off. It is up to you, then, to plead my case, and I would consider it a great favor if you did so.

With that in mind, I put on my glasses, take up my pen, and begin:

Franklin "Freekin" Ripp was born in the town of Snickering Willows, which was founded in 1889 by Horatio Snickering III. Mr. Snickering was the inventor of Mystery Meat, that strange gray mass which you no doubt have eaten in your school cafeteria. Possibly, like my young niece Belle, you declared yourself a vegetarian after the fact.

(A word on Belle: She is staying with me for the weekend so that her parents might have a break, and has asked if she might observe my narration of this stirring and exciting story. Since I am a very indulgent uncle, I have consented. I doubt she can do much harm, and we in the Narrating business find that upon occasion, a second set of eyes can spot some trifling matter such as a misplaced comma or a wayward question mark. So she has poured herself cocoa in a mug with fairies painted on it, taken up her sparkly pen topped with a bright green feather—Belle, please mind the jam on your fingers—and

settled in quite nicely on a lacquered Chinese chair beside my own. So there it is, and on we go.)

Whatever your feelings about Mystery Meat, it was an overnight sensation in 1889. Horatio Snickering III became a millionaire and the little village of Snickering Willows ballooned into a town. A huge brick factory replaced the tiny kitchen where Mr. Snickering had concocted the first batch of Mystery Meat. Those sprawling buildings steamed, smoked, and clanked twenty-four hours a day, seven days a week, churning out the key to Snickering Willows's success.

As soon as Mystery Meat hit the shelves, jealous rivals tried to duplicate the Ultra Top Secret Recipe so they could make their own imitation products. Horatio Snickering III was the only person who knew exactly what was in it, and so the secret formula was safe . . . for the time being. But he knew very well that if he wanted Mystery Meat to outlive himself, he would have to pass the recipe on, and *that* person would have to pass the recipe on, and so forth.

Now, you may recall that old saying by Benjamin Franklin: "Three can keep a secret, if two of them are dead." As Mr. Snickering was a businessman, he knew exactly how devious businesspeople could be. He worried that someone, somewhere, would manage to pry the

4

secret out of one of his unsuspecting secret-keepers.

For example, someone might say, "Here is a list of one thousand ingredients I am allergic to. Are any of them in Mystery Meat, and, if so, which ones, and in what amounts?"

Or, "If I give you three million dollars and a mansion, will you give me the recipe for Mystery Meat?"

Or, "As I have kidnapped your wife and child, would you be so kind as to give me the formula for Mystery Meat, so that I may return them to you unharmed?"

Horatio Snickering III became convinced that one of his secret-keepers would crack under such questioning. It kept him up nights. Some claimed it drove him insane. The only solution he could devise was to make all questions illegal. Anyone found guilty of asking any question, no matter how seemingly slight or innocent, would be escorted to the Snickering Willows city limits, forbidden ever to return.

He had the power to make such a decree because he owned the town of Snickering Willows lock, stock, and barrel. He owned all the buildings and all the major businesses. So the people who refused to obey the new law either moved away or got sent away. After a couple of generations, Snickering Willowites pretty much forgot *how* to ask questions.

I pause a moment here to inform you that I just read this thrilling portion of my exciting tale aloud to Belle, and she has informed me that it is *boring*. She says I'm going on too long. Perhaps she has a point. I feel I have so much more to explain, but perhaps it's best to stand aside and leap into the story itself. So let me boil it down for you:

1. Franklin Ripp died because he failed to ask the question that would have saved his life. Since I cannot reveal how he died, I cannot tell you what that question was. It may have been, "Is it really safe to skateboard in the dark without a helmet?" Or perhaps, "If I swallow all this candy and drink this fizzy soda, will my stomach explode?" Or even, "Has anyone *ever* survived this?"

2. When Franklin discovered that he had died, he was naturally very upset. He badgered the Afterlife Commission over and over again with the first question he had ever asked: "WHY NOW?" He insisted that he had been about to have a wonderful life, and that it was cut short most unfairly.

3. Monsieur DeMise, a member of the Commission, agreed with Franklin. A very romantic and sentimental being, he realized that Franklin was haunted by his love for the beautiful Lilly Weezbrock. Franklin had very nearly kissed Lilly the day before he died, but at the

last moment, he lost his nerve. This, Monsieur DeMise believed, was the very reason Franklin could not accept his death. Monsieur DeMise insisted that Franklin deserved a second chance at life—in order to claim that kiss.

4. Ms. Totenbone, the head of the Afterlife Commission, finally consented to send Franklin back—on one condition. If by the end of the school year—June thirteenth, the anniversary of his death—he had not kissed Lilly, he would leave the Land of the Living forever.

5. Franklin was sent back to the Land of the Living in his decomposing body, and continued to rot. As soon as he set foot in school, he was nicknamed "Freekin" by his nemesis, Brad Anderwater.

6. Freekin's two best friends from the Afterlife came with him to Snickering Willows. Their names are Pretty and Scary, and they are actually monsters from the Underworld, which is a special part of the Afterlife reserved for monsters, ghouls, fiends, the occasional shape-shifting phantom, and all manner of freaks of nature—

OMG, everyone, Belle here! Just turn the page already and we'll get straight to the point before my uncle bores you to death.

Chapter One:
In Which Our Hero Suffers!

"Uh-oh, Freekin. Mommy so boo-hoo-hoo," Pretty murmured as she raised herself up on the tips of her tentacles and peered through the frosty panes of the Ripp family's dining room window. She anxiously clacked her many tiny fangs, her ponytail ears bobbing in the falling snow, and Freekin ticked his glance downward to make sure she hadn't started gnawing on

the windowsill. When Pretty was nervous, she chewed on things. She also chewed on things when she was happy.

Freekin's mother sat hunched at the dining room table, clutching a very official-looking document in her trembling hands. While Mrs. Ripp cried, Mr. Ripp paced and gestured wildly as he talked on the phone. His words were muffled by the thickness of the window Freekin was peering through.

Crying harder, Freekin's mom unfolded the document. Freekin pressed his nose to the glass and squinted at the elegant letters sprawling across the paper:

HOUSE ARREST DECREE FOR FRANKLIN RIPP

CRIME: CURIOSITY

Oh no. I'm doomed, Freekin thought. He was flooded with fear and shame. In Snickering Willows, it was worse to be curious than to be murderous. He was sure that right now, his parents were wishing he had never come back from the dead. He almost—but not quite—felt that way, too.

"Freekin's mommy crying why?" Pretty asked him. She hadn't been brought up in Snickering Willows, so to her, it was quite normal to ask questions.

"I'm in trouble," he told her. If his heart could still beat, it would have been hammering against the calcifying bones of his chest. If he could still sweat, his clothes would have been as wet as a morgue sheet after a particularly grisly autopsy. But he could still tremble, and he shook as if he were having a severe attack of rigor mortis. "Principal Lugosi must have reported me to the police, like he threatened."

"Bad man. Eat his eyeballs," Pretty grunted, clenching her fists.

"I should never have asked Mr. Lugosi a question." Freekin bent over and soothed Sophie, his dog, with a little scratch behind her ears. "But I had no choice. People all over town are coming down with Chronic Snickering Syndrome. I had to ask him if he knew what was causing it."

Freekin clenched his jagged teeth. "He said people were getting it because they were allergic to me. Because I'm undead. But I know he's wrong. Steve's cousin in Minnesota has it, and he's never met me."

"*Wahwah*," Scary murmured. The little shape-shifting phantom perched on Freekin's shoulder and wrapped his wing around Freekin's head. He patted Freekin's cheek and cooed with sympathy.

"*Woof*," Sophie chuffed, shifting her weight in the snow.

Freekin's mom raised her head as if she had heard the dog. Freekin darted away from the window, gesturing

for his friends to do the same. The snow-choked sky was dark, so there was very little threat that she would see them, but Freekin wasn't taking any chances. So far, his caution had paid off: Pretty and Scary had lived in his bedroom for almost a month, and his parents had no idea they were there.

The Ripps assumed the dozen or so cats who had moved in were Freekin's new pets. They would have let him raise rattlesnakes if he'd wanted to, they were so happy to have him back among the living. But the cats belonged to Pretty. They adored her.

A moment, please? This is Belle again. Uncle, you're still not getting on with it.

Knowing that he had better get on with it, Freekin turned to his two best friends.

"Go on up to my room," he said. "I'm going to talk to my parents."

"*Aleekileeki*," Scary said, squeezing Freekin more tightly and shaking his head.

"Go on. I'll be okay," Freekin assured them.

"Me so hoping," Pretty answered earnestly, gazing up at him with her seven eyes.

Pretty scampered away across the snowy yard, Scary fluttering behind her, and slithered up the bare-branched tree that led to Freekin's bedroom window. Sophie stuck

11

close to Freekin, and boy and dog entered the house together through the front door.

"Franklin!" his mother called.

"Yeah, Mom, it's me," he called back.

"*Woof*," Sophie said.

Mrs. Ripp hurried out of the dining room and met him in the entryway. Her face was swollen with tears, and he felt terrible because he knew he had caused them. When she threw her arms around him and held him close, he felt even worse.

"Oh, sweetheart, there's been such a horrible mistake," she began. "Mr. Lugosi accused you of doing something very, very wrong. But don't worry, honey. Your dad's on the phone with the best defense lawyer in Snickering Willows, and she'll be able to get the charges dropped. Then the Mystery Meat factory will give your dad his job back and everything will be just fine."

"Are you sure, Mom? Are you sure everything will be fine?"

His mother jerked away from him and stared. All the color drained from her face, until she was as pale as Freekin's friend Raven, the king of the goths of Snickering Willows.

Freekin shut his eyes tightly. He had just asked a question in front of his own mother.

"Mom, I'm sorry," he said, reaching a hand out to her.

She maintained her distance, swaying as if she were about to faint. "Franklin, we raised you to be better than that," she said in a choked voice. "Our ancestors have lived in Snickering Willows since 1902, and no one has *ever* . . . asked . . . a . . . question." He could see that it was difficult for her to even form the words.

"Okay, it's all settled," Mr. Ripp announced, joining his wife and son in the foyer. Obviously unaware of what had just happened, he beamed at them, flipped his phone shut, and put it in the pocket of his gray trousers. "Ms. Savini is worth every penny we're paying her. She just told me that the judge in Franklin's case has agreed to order Mr. Lugosi to take a hearing test. She's confident that will clear up this misunderstanding."

"Honey, it's not a misunderstanding," Mrs. Ripp got out. Then she choked back a sob and rushed past Freekin, dashing up the stairs. Freekin heard her footfalls overhead, and then the slam of the master bedroom door.

Mr. Ripp frowned at Freekin. "Your mother's awfully upset," he said slowly. That was how people asked questions in Snickering Willows. They made observations. They hinted.

Then they waited for answers.

Freekin hung his head. "Dad, Mr. Lugosi's hearing is fine. I *did* ask a question. In fact, I've asked more than one."

"*Franklin*." His dad's voice was a hoarse whisper. He went gray, and his face sagged. He seemed to age before Freekin's very eyes.

"I know it goes against our traditions," Freekin began.

"Franklin, it's against the law! It's indecent!" Mr. Ripp buried his face in his hands. "We failed you. We tried to be good parents, raise you up to be a good member of the community. But somewhere, we went wrong."

"Dad, so many people are getting sick. Don't you wonder why? Don't you want to know how to stop it?"

"Oh, Franklin, please, please, no more." Mr. Ripp covered his ears and turned away.

"Dad, I *died* because I didn't ask questions," Freekin pressed. "Horatio Snickering III was wrong to make questions illegal. They're normal. They're good."

He was greeted by dead silence as his father kept his back to him. Mr. Ripp's shoulders began to shake with silent weeping. Then he cleared his throat. "Son, don't ever say anything like that out loud again."

"I'm sorry, but—"

Mr. Ripp turned around. "They're going to put you

on trial. You know what they'll do to you if you confess to Curiosity."

"They'll send me away," Freekin said brokenly. "I'll never see you or Mom or Sophie again." *Or Lilly. I'll never get the chance to kiss her. Then on June thirteenth, I'll have to leave the Land of the Living forever.*

"Oh, you'll see us," his father said. "We'll go with you."

"No, you can't, Dad," Freekin said, alarmed. "I won't let you!"

"It's not up for discussion," Mr. Ripp replied. "We're your parents, and we won't let you go alone." He sounded like he was a million years old. "I'm going upstairs to comfort your mother."

※ ※ ※

Freekin's trial date was set for two weeks later. He couldn't leave the house, and he felt like he would go crazy from the tension and the boredom. He thought a million times about sneaking out and trying to talk to Lilly, but he didn't want to cause more trouble for his parents. Pretty and Scary tried to entertain him, and his friends Steve and Raven stayed in touch via e-mail. Freekin was grateful to them, but he felt as if he had been buried alive.

On the night before his trial, Freekin was so nervous that all he could do was pace back and forth across his room with Scary perched on his shoulder. Pretty trundled after him, all her cats crowding around her and batting at her tentacles.

"Bad men hurt Freekin, tra la la," she sang grimly to herself as she clacked her teeth. "Eat their eyeballs, tra la la la."

An instant message alert chimed on Freekin's desktop computer, and he glanced over at the monitor to see who it was.

SK8BOARDER STEVE: Hey, Freekin, hope U R doing OK.

Freekin smiled pensively. Steve had been his best friend since kindergarten. They skateboarded together. They had a band called the 50-50s, named after a totally awesome skateboarding stunt. After Freekin died, he'd missed his old friend like crazy. It would hurt just as badly if he had to say good-bye for a second time.

He sat down to type.

FREEKIN: Thx, Steve.

SK8BOARDER STEVE: Trying 2 come 2morrow 2 trial.

FREEKIN: Don't get in trouble.

SK8BOARDER STEVE: Freekin, YER my homey!

Freekin's instant messaging alert sounded again. Raven had come online.

DEATHBEPROUD: Freekin, I send good wishes from the goth community.

The goths had treated Freekin like a rock star ever since he had come back from the grave.

FREEKIN: Thx, Raven. How is Shadesse?

DEATHBEPROUD: They say her case of CSS is the worst one yet.

FREEKIN: ☹ Hope she gets better soon.

DEATHBEPROUD: That would be good. However, we all sicken. Death comes for us all.

Freekin was grateful for Raven's friendship and the support of his faithful goth-minions. After Steve, they had been the first kids to welcome him back to the Land of the Living.

SK8BOARDER STEVE: Yo, F, check out the pic I just sent you!

Freekin opened his e-mail inbox and clicked on a new message from Steve. There was a picture of big, tall Steve, rail-thin Raven, and Raven's pale second-in-command, the goth named Tuberculosis. All three were wearing black T-shirts with the words FREE FREEKIN! in white letters.

"I have such great friends," Freekin said to Pretty,

who had plopped down on the floor among her kitties and begun gnawing on an old scratching post like a piece of corn on the cob.

"Pretty is great friend," she assured him as she picked splinters out of her mouth. "Scary is great friend."

"*Zibu*," Scary said, morphing into a Valentine's heart.

Freekin ticked his glance over to the wall covered with pictures of Lilly. If he had to leave, he would miss her most of all. He would never stop missing her, ever.

He got up and resumed his pacing.

"Bad men, bad men, tra la la," Pretty sang. "Eat their eyeballs, tra la la la."

Chapter Two:
In Which Our Hero Stands Trial!

✳—✳—✳

At daybreak on the morning of his trial, Freekin put on the new suit his mom had bought for him. Pretty looked him up and down. As did the cat on her shoulder, the other on her head, and the five or six batting at her tentacles. Scary fluttered around him for a quick inspection, then gave him a butterfly kiss on his cheek.

"You so pretty," Pretty informed him sweetly. She

smoothed down her jumper with the dead bunny head on it and gave her ponytail ears a little shake. "Me so pretty." Her voice was a soft coo.

"Thank you, Pretty. And yes, you are very pretty," Freekin agreed. He took a deep breath. "So, you understand that this may be it? We may have to leave Snickering Willows and never, ever come back." Just saying the words made him panicky.

Pretty frowned and clacked her fangs. "Bad men. Eat their eyeballs. Blow fire on them. Burn them up."

"No, Pretty," Freekin said. "Remember. No matter what, you can't do any of that."

"Franklin, sweetheart!" His mother knocked on his door.

"Just a sec, Mom," he said in a loud voice. "Okay, go out the window," he whispered to Pretty and Scary. "Wait for me outside the courthouse." He handed Pretty a printout of the Snickering Willows Hall of Justice, complete with street directions and a map. "Don't go inside." He remembered the ruckus they had caused at his hearing with the Afterlife Commission. It could only be worse here in the Land of the Living, where the wheels of justice had never run into monsters or phantoms—so to speak.

"Pretty waits. Scary waits," she assured him, all seven

of her eyes welling up as she gazed at him. She flopped all her tentacles, one over another, the way someone else might cross her fingers. "Me so hoping."

"Me too." He pointed to the window. "I'll see you later."

As Freekin's parents drove him to the courthouse in their highly uncool minivan, the gray, pollution-saturated snow coagulated on the rooftops and treetops of Snickering Willows like a layer of half-frozen Mystery Meat. It was an ominous reminder of the power of Horatio Snickering III—although he had been dead for over a hundred years, his laws still governed the behavior of every single person in Snickering Willows, and woe to anyone who broke those laws.

On the snowy courthouse steps, a cluster of reporters and a TV crew craned their necks and swiveled their cameras as the Ripps drove slowly up. Hardly anyone got arrested for Curiosity anymore, and Freekin's trial was big news.

Mr. Ripp parked in one of the stalls marked RESERVED FOR THE ACCUSED and Freekin opened his door.

"Shoo, beat it!" Freekin's attorney Ms. Savini ordered the reporters as she pushed through the little crowd. She

was wearing a severe black suit and heeled boots, and she was very thin and wiry. "My client has no comment."

"Just one quick observation." A heavyset man waved a tape recorder at Freekin. "Tell us what's going through your mind right now. Thoughts of despair, doom, desperation."

"Ignore him. He's an idiot," Ms. Savini told Freekin. Her heels clattered as she came up beside him and slammed his car door shut for him. His dazed, frightened parents were climbing out of the front seat. Slightly behind Ms. Savini, a man in a dark blue police officer's uniform gestured at the reporters to disperse.

"Judge Englund says you can talk to the accused after the sentence is passed," the police officer told them.

"I thought he was innocent until proven guilty," Mrs. Ripp said in an agonized tone of voice.

"He is, he is," Ms. Savini assured her. She turned to Freekin. "Okay, Creakin, let's run through our game plan one more time." She grabbed his arm, then grimaced slightly and let go of it. She gestured for Freekin to follow her toward the steps. "You're pleading innocent. You never asked questions and you never will."

"It's Freekin. But I *did* ask questions," he reminded her as he hurried to keep up. "I did it because—"

She cut him off with a shake of her head. "We've been

through this." She sounded very frustrated. "There will be no admission of guilt, *none*. I went that route with a client once, tried to get him off with a plea of insanity."

She shook her head at Mr. and Mrs. Ripp, who walked at her side. "Five minutes after the trial, he was gone forever. That's why I insist upon being paid in advance," she added. "Not that I think your kid is going anywhere. But you have a much better chance of that if we stay away from the insanity defense."

"But what's insane is *not* asking questions," Freekin insisted.

His mother shuddered and buried her face in her hands. His father put his arm around her and patted her. They shuffled up the steps together, bent over and miserable.

"Holy cow, don't go there," Ms. Savini ordered him, rolling her eyes. "Look at your parents. Look how upset they are. You're questioning the basic values this town holds dear. The jury will eat you for breakfast."

Then she got quiet. "The *jury*," she repeated, as if to herself. "The jury." She grinned at him. "Leakin, I think I just figured out how to save you. Come on." At her nod, the officer opened the heavy wooden door to the courthouse with a flourish.

"It's Freekin," Freekin corrected her, walking through the door. "How?"

"For the love of Mike, shut up with the questions," she snapped at him as she clacked down a tiled hall lined with oil portraits of men and women in judicial robes. "Come on." She reached for the brass doorknob of a door labeled COURTROOM NO. 13. "Leave the talking to me."

Freekin walked in a daze into the dark and dreary courtroom and scanned the rows of observers. He knew he had been foolish to hope Lilly might show up. Steve and his skateboarding friends Hal and Otter were there, wearing FREE FREEKIN! T-shirts. So was Coach Karloff, with six members of the football team, including Sam Sontgerath, Brian Vernia, and Jesse Greenfield. They really needed Freekin for the team. Raven, Tuberculosis, and at least a dozen goths were there, all in their black T-shirts. There were other people Freekin didn't recognize. Some of them were quite old, and they looked like they wanted to hang him on the spot. They must have been there to make sure justice was served.

Freekin's parents trailed behind him and Ms. Savini. They both stopped at the first row of seats. Freekin's mom sniffled into a tissue, then leaned forward and kissed his cheek.

"It's going to be all right," she said, even though she looked as if she were about to break down sobbing.

"We're here for you," his dad added, giving him a tight hug.

"C'mon," Ms. Savini said.

There were two tables at the front of the room. The prosecuting attorney's name was Mr. Carpenter. The dour, bald man sat at a cloth-covered table on Freekin's left. His nose was red and bulbous—two of the early symptoms of Chronic Snickering Syndrome. The raised dais topped with the judge's desk loomed at the end of the courtroom. There was a witness box to the judge's left, and then, the jury.

Yikes. Twelve men and women sat in two rows, and all of them were glaring at Freekin. One old lady was holding her nose. Okay, he *did* have a little bit of an odor problem. Decomposition could do that to a person.

"All rise for the Honorable Judge Englund. Court is now in session!" said the tall officer in the dark blue uniform. Then he sneezed as a pale, thin man swept into the dark and dreary wood-paneled courtroom.

"Please be seated," the judge told the courtroom.

As Freekin obeyed, he heard the flopping of tentacles and fierce whispering. Oh no! Pretty and Scary had snuck into the courtroom. He looked left and right, searching for them.

Then someone tapped the tip of his toe.

"La la la," that same someone whispered. It was Pretty, of course. Freekin shut his eyes tightly and balled his fists inside his pants pockets.

Don't make a scene, he silently begged them.

"This is the case of the people of Snickering Willows versus Franklin Ripp," the judge said. He looked hard at Freekin, and Freekin shriveled inside. He felt butterflies dancing in his stomach. Or maybe they were blowflies.

The tension inside the courtroom was so thick, it could be cut with a scalpel. Freekin heard his mother crying. Underneath the table, Pretty began to gnaw on the table's wooden leg.

I can't believe this is happening, Freekin thought. *I never dreamed I would be sitting in a courtroom, wondering if I only had six more months to be here. Asking questions. Hurting my parents. Scaring Lilly away.*

He hung his head.

"It's gonna be okay, Reekin," Ms. Savini muttered under her breath. Then she raised her chin. "Your Honor, if I may address the jury."

"Very well." The judge inclined his head.

Ms. Savini got to her feet. The rest of the courtroom strained forward as she swept around the table and walked over to the jury.

"Your Honor, ladies and gentlemen, in our great nation, the legal system allows us to be judged by a jury of our peers." Ms. Savini waved a hand at the jury box.

Many of them had red, swollen noses. "By 'peers,' we mean people who are like us. People who can judge if we are obeying the laws of our society because they are also members of that society."

She smiled at the jurors. The old lady sniffed behind a handkerchief. The others stared back at Ms. Savini with narrowed eyes, as if she were as guilty of wrongdoing as Freekin.

"Peers. That's correct," Judge Englund said, shifting impatiently.

Ms. Savini walked right over to the jury box and put her hands on the railing. "*Achoo!* Pardon me. My point is, these wonderful people are *not* my client's peers." She smiled at each one as if to take the sting out of what she was saying. "They're all living human beings. And my client, Franklin Ripp, is undead."

"Objection, Your Honor!" Mr. Carpenter jumped to his feet. "That's ridiculous."

"Grrr," Pretty growled beneath the table. A tentacle poked out and slithered toward the man. Freekin nudged it back under the table with the tip of his shoe.

"No, it's not ridiculous. It's true. Franklin is undead," Ms. Savini shot back, wiping her nose.

"But that does not excuse him from obeying the law," Mr. Carpenter insisted.

"But it *does* prevent him from getting a fair trial," Ms. Savini argued, crossing her arms as she lifted her chin. They glared at each other, neither one blinking. Then Mr. Carpenter sneezed.

"Bless you," Ms. Savini said graciously.

"Woodiwoodi," Scary whispered from beneath the table.

Then Judge Englund sneezed three times, coughed twice, and cleared his throat.

"You have a point, Ms. Savini," he said. He looked from Freekin to the jury and back again. The old lady on the jury frowned. Clearly, she wanted to find Freekin guilty.

Ms. Savini sneezed. Mr. Carpenter sneezed.

A few of the people in the audience behind Freekin sneezed and blew their noses. There were no other sounds, until Mrs. Ripp began crying again.

Freekin was so nervous, he would have held his breath if he could still breathe.

He distinctly heard gnawing on the table leg.

"Very well." The judge picked up his gavel. "By the power vested in me, I declare this a mistrial. Franklin Ripp, you are free to go." He slammed the gavel down on his desk.

Cheers and applause rose up behind Freekin. But there were also groans, and lots of muttering.

"Franklin!" Mrs. Ripp scooted around Ms. Savini,

rushed toward her son, and threw her arms around him. His father followed right behind her, slapping Freekin on the back and gathering him up in a big hug.

Leaping to their feet, Steve, Hal, and Otter pumped their arms and bellowed, "Yo, Free-kin!" Raven actually smiled and inclined his head. That was as close to joy as a goth could get and still maintain his dignity.

"Thank you, thank you!" Mr. Ripp said, shaking Ms. Savini's hand. "That was amazing!"

"It's why I make the big bucks," she said proudly. She cocked her head at Freekin as she held her handkerchief to her nose. "You're going to be okay now, kid, as long as you don't . . . do anything drastic." She patted him on the shoulder, then grimaced slightly and pulled her hand away. He checked the shoulder of his suit. Some guys had to worry about dandruff; he had to worry about maggots.

"Come on, sweetie, let's get out of here," Freekin's mom said, lacing her fingers with Freekin's and urging him out of the courtroom.

He looked back over his shoulder to the defense table. Pretty and Scary had not yet emerged.

"Um, I think I dropped something," he said, giving her a look. Since on occasion his ears or fingers came off, it made perfect sense.

"Okay, hurry," she urged him.

He hurried back and dropped to his knee. He lifted the tablecloth to see Pretty and Scary hugging each other and dancing in a circle.

"Hey, guys," he said. "Pretty, you sneaky little monster. I *told* you to wait outside." He tried to sound stern, but he couldn't stay mad at them.

"Me so happy!" Pretty shrieked. Scary transformed into a big hand and covered her mouth. Her seven eyes spun.

"Me too," Freekin told her. "Really happy." He yanked on her ponytail. "Can you guys sneak out the same way you snuck in?"

Behind Scary's big hand, Pretty nodded.

"Good. I'll meet you back at our house." He grinned, got to his feet, and headed for his parents. His mom was beaming at him.

Freekin smiled a blindingly bright smile at his parents. "Let's get out of here."

"Yee-ha!" his mother said happily.

"I second that yee-ha," his dad added.

Arm in arm, the Ripps left the courtroom.

Chapter Three:
In Which Pretty Makes an Interesting Discovery!

* * *

"Look at that crowd. Some highly dangerous criminal must be on trial," Deirdre said to Lilly as the two best friends tromped through the snow. On their way back from the Horatio Snickering III Municipal Library, they were strolling on the sidewalk opposite the Snickering Willows Hall of Justice. A mob of reporters and onlookers mingled at the foot of the stairs leading to

the entrance, and a cordon of Snickering Willows Police Department officers was holding them back.

Lilly felt as if she had swallowed the unabridged Oxford English Dictionary. She knew exactly what it was all about. Today was Freekin's Curiosity trial. She never dreamed it would be over so soon, or she never would have risked walking right past the courthouse and running into him.

As if on cue, an ecstatic Freekin, his happy parents, and his cheering friends burst through the door. Freekin stood at the top of the stairs and flung his arms over his head.

"Free-kin! Free-kin!" a throng of football players and skateboarders chanted and whooped. Raven and his goths stood by, almost smiling.

"Oh, wow, it's him," Deirdre said. "He must have been declared innocent of you-know-what."

"Curiosity," Lilly said, taking a perverse pleasure in saying the word aloud. *I don't know how he could be found innocent. I heard him asking questions with my own ears. And criticizing me for not asking questions. Trying to get me to break the law.*

But she didn't say anything aloud. She didn't trust herself to speak. She was all jumbled up inside.

She stole a glance at him, only to find him staring at her.

Heat rose to her cheeks; she clenched her jaw and lowered her head.

"Let's turn around, Deirdre," she said through gritted teeth.

"Lilly, it's okay," Deirdre said. "Just keep walking. He's across the street. There's no way he can hassle you."

Lilly started to walk faster and almost slipped on the ice. Glancing up through her lashes, she saw Freekin take a step in her direction, and she inhaled sharply. She walked faster. She and Freekin were *over*. Forever.

Pretty and Scary gave each other one last hug; then they peered out beneath the tablecloth to see if anyone was still in the room. It was empty. Just to be on the safe side, Scary changed into a wheeled trashcan—the same disguise he had devised to sneak into the courtroom in the first place.

Pretty lifted the lid and tumbled inside, giggling as Scary began to roll up the aisle. He pushed the door open and they wheeled into the courthouse lobby. It was very grand, with marble floors, stone columns, and a statue of a blindfolded woman holding a pair of scales. Her name was Justice.

Scary resumed his normal shape, and the two friends crept behind a row of grand columns as they searched

the throng for Freekin. Pretty spotted him standing in the opened door of the main entrance. Framed by light, he looked like a handsome prince.

"Freekin!" she screamed, completely forgetting that she and Scary were sneaking. She was so happy, she started turning on her own axis, spinning around five or six times like a gyroscope. Scary flew after her, pulling her ear, trying to slow her down.

"There are no pets allowed in the courthouse," a security guard announced as he hurried toward them. Pretty darted on ahead, weaving her way through the legs of the human beings. Scary changed into a dog collar around her neck and went along for the ride.

"Freekin!" she shrieked again, only at a far less ear-piercing volume. Still, her voice echoed off the stone columns and marble floors.

Couldn't he hear her? Everybody else could. People were bending down, calling, "Here, doggie. Here, girl." Ha! Like she would fall for *that*!

Finally she scuttled up behind her boy. But he still didn't notice her. He was staring at something in the distance.

Pretty looked in the same direction.

Lilly.

Grrrr. Pretty glared at the perky blond cheerleader

walking down the other side of the street with that Deirdre girl. Lilly had on a dark blue coat and dark blue boots and they made her eyes look very blue, and Pretty knew Freekin's favorite color was blue (because she knew everything there was to know about her Freekin). And Freekin loved Lilly's blue eyes, but so what? The stupid, yucky human girl only had two. Pretty had *seven*.

"Lilly?" Freekin called, but his voice was just a whisper. "Do you think she's smiling at me?" he asked his friend Steve.

"Freekin, chill. You just nearly got run out of town for, y'know, *asking questions*," Steve whispered, nudging him with his elbow. "And you cannot seriously like a chick who would dump you for a jerk like Brad Anderwater."

"I see no smile," Raven informed Freekin.

"Hiya, Freekin. Knock-knock," Pretty whispered, tugging on his pants leg.

"Yeah, I *can* like her. And I do," Freekin said. "Seriously. I'll never stop liking her, Steve. Ever."

"The matters of the heart can be dark and dreary," Raven offered sympathetically.

"No kidding." Freekin walked on. Pretty's fingertips lost their grip on his pants leg and he kept going without even noticing. He started down the stairs.

Tears welled in all of her eyes. *Why? Why Lilly?* she

thought miserably. *Why not Pretty?*

"Knock-knock?" she tried again, watching as he walked to his parents' car and climbed inside.

"Wahwah, Pretty," Scary said, giving her neck a squeeze.

"BWAH!" Pretty bellowed, and she fled the courthouse.

<hr />

Pretty trundled all over Snickering Willows in a panic born of grief. She was so upset she paid no attention to where she was going. She just waddled along like a brokenhearted armored tank, dimly aware of car brakes and car horns.

"Wahwah," Scary soothed her.

Why? Why does Freekin like Yucky Lilly?

Tears streamed down her face, soaking the dead bunny head on her jumper. She orbited the municipal park, crying her eyes out—literally. Scary popped back into his regular shape and flitted after them, gathering them all up and helping her put them back in.

She'd been so deliriously happy about the outcome of the trial, and then he just walked away like she didn't even exist . . . like she didn't matter at all, and she was just . . . so . . .

So . . .

She kept going, until the air grew cooler and she heard the familiar *squeeeak* of rusty iron. Smelled the familiar scent of damp earth. Heard an owl hoot. Tripped over a slab of cement jutting straight up from the ground.

They were in the Snickering Willows Cemetery, where she, Freekin, and Scary had come back from the Afterlife. Gripped with memories, she started crying all over again. Her vision blurred from the sheer volume of tears.

Then trundle, trundle, trundle, *clunk*.

Pretty tumbled forward into a big, deep ditch. "AIIIEE!" she cried as Scary turned into an air bag and cushioned her fall.

She caught her breath. "Scary is okay?"

"*Zibu,*" he assured her, crumpled up beneath her. Since he was a shape-shifting phantom, he didn't get hurt very often.

She looked around. There was no one else inside the ditch, not even a dead boy.

She pushed herself up to a standing position and looked up at the headstone, high above them on a rounded mound of grass.

SWEENY BURTON

R.I.P.

BELOVED FRIEND

DATE OF DEATH

AUGUST 31ST

August thirty-first was just one week before Freekin had come back from the Afterlife. Freekin was not all that rotten. So the dead boy should still be here. How had the body decomposed so fast?

"He so bye-bye, Scary," she said, feeling with her tentacles for a skull or a knucklebone or *something*. "No coffin. No body. No slime. No bones."

"Hey, you kids shouldn't be playing in the graveyard!" someone called from above.

"Uh-oh," Pretty whispered as she and Scary gazed upward, through the broken slats of wood. Hands on his hips, a man in a pair of overalls was peering into the grave. He had a shovel in his hand.

"Grrowf, woof-woof!" she said. Even though it hurt her feelings, she usually got in less trouble if people thought she was a dog.

"Oh, hey, puppy," the man said, more gently. "You must've fallen, little feller, but you don't look hurt."

"Yip-yip-yip!" Pretty cried. Then she leaped out of the empty grave, dashed between the man's legs, and shot back the way she had come, through the rusty iron-gated entrance of the cemetery. Scary fluttered into the darkness just above her head.

"Here, doggie!" The man snapped his fingers. "I'll take you home until we find your owner."

"Pretty *goes* home," she murmured. Home to Freekin, who, she hoped, had forgotten all about that stupid, ugly, dumbo two-eyed Lilly by now.

Fresh tears dripped down her face and clung to the tips of her fangs like melting icicles.

"Grrr, eat her eyeballs," she muttered.

"Wahwah, Pretty," Scary replied.

When she reached the Ripp home, Pretty slithered up the old oak tree while Scary opened the window. Freekin was sitting on his bed strumming his guitar. He smiled when he saw them, then laid down the guitar, stood up, and opened his arms.

"Guys! Where'd you go?" he said. "I was worried!"

Oh! How wonderful!

Delighted, Pretty dried all her eyes and trundled over to him. She hugged him tightly, and he hugged her back while Scary gave him a butterfly kiss on the cheek.

"Oh, Freekin, me so happy," she whispered, nuzzling his hand. "Happy, happy, happy!" She did a little dance on the tips of her tentacles.

"Me too, Pretty," he replied, giving one of her ponytail ears an affectionate tug. She giggled.

And she was so ecstatic that she forgot all about telling him about the empty grave.

The next morning, Freekin jerked his head up at the knock on his door. Since he'd been expelled from school, his parents had let him sleep as late as he wanted—never realizing that their undead son didn't need to sleep at all.

"Franklin, wake up. Good news," his father said as he cracked open the door. He was all dressed up. A trio of kittens batted at his shiny shoe.

"Hi, Dad," Freekin said, moving a fluffy sable-colored cat off his chest as he sat up. He glanced around the room to check if Pretty's usual nighttime nest of towels was visible. She lay snoring at the foot of his bed, snuggled up with some of her cats. Fast-thinking Scary turned into a pile of dirty laundry and completely covered the little sleeping monster.

Freekin's dad eased the door open gingerly. "Principal Lugosi called. You're cleared to return to school."

"No way!" Freekin cried. His entire mind filled with an image of Lilly. Now that he was cleared, maybe they could get back together again.

His dad grinned. "Yes, way. He said to show up on time today or face detention. That sounds like the Principal Lugosi we both know."

"Yeah, it does," Freekin said. He'd have to be careful

around him. He was under no illusion that Principal Lugosi would be glad that he was back.

His dad's smile got bigger. "*And* I've got a job interview."

Freekin's mouth dropped open. "Dad, that is seriously awesome!"

"It's at Rigortoni's Pizza Parlor," Mr. Ripp said. "They need a new manager." He stood a little straighter. "You know, I've worked my whole adult life at the Mystery Meat factory. I'm looking forward to trying something different."

Freekin sagged with relief. His family had had a close call because of him. But things were definitely looking more hopeful.

"So get dressed and come on down to breakfast," his dad told him. "You can't be late for school, and I can't be late for my interview."

Freekin showered and slathered himself with deodorant. Then he put on a pair of jeans, a dark blue T-shirt, and a black sweater.

Downstairs in the dining room, Mrs. Ripp had breakfast waiting for him. She still hadn't noticed that he never ate.

His beloved dog, Sophie, was planted beneath his chair. She raised her head and thumped her tail in anticipation of the savory tidbits Freekin would hand down to her.

"This is such wonderful news," his mom said. Then she sneezed hard. "Excuse me."

Freekin studied her. Was *she* coming down with Chronic Snickering Syndrome?

I have to figure this out, he thought with a renewed sense of urgency. *I'll just have to go about it very quietly.*

They ate. Or rather, Freekin's parents ate, and he fed Sophie. Then he went upstairs to grab his backpack. He bent down beside the "pile of dirty laundry," lifted up a pillow case—in reality, Scary's wing—and planted a soft kiss on Pretty's cheek.

"See you guys this afternoon," he whispered.

"Oh, Freekin, bye-bye," Pretty murmured, half asleep, but radiant with joy.

Her Freekin had kissed her!

"You've got to be the luckiest juvenile delinquent in the world, Ripp," Principal Lugosi said before he launched into a sneezing fit. The principal's nose was extremely swollen and very, very red. Freekin tried not to stare at it as the man doubled over, sniffling and hacking. He waited politely while Principal Lugosi grabbed several tissues from the box on his desk and blew his nose.

He honked like a goose.

"You managed to go free after breaking the most sacred law we have in Snickering Willows," the man said, tossing the used tissues into his trash can. "And now you get to come back to school."

Freekin stayed silent. Clearly, Principal Lugosi wasn't done ranting at him.

"The *only* reason I'm letting you back in is Coach Karloff asked me as a personal favor. Seems you're the team's secret weapon. This year we beat the Snorting Cypresses Body Snatchers, and we haven't defeated them in years."

It was true. Freekin *was* the team's secret weapon. He could be disassembled, but he couldn't be injured. He could be tackled a dozen times in a row and never need a time-out. And he never got tired. He could run up and down the field for the entire game without breaking a sweat. (He didn't sweat anymore, either.)

"But hear me, Ripp." Principal Lugosi wagged a finger in Freekin's face. "I don't want you here. You're trouble. And not only because of the question asking. I still think people are allergic to you. I'm convinced you're the cause of Chronic Snickering Syndrome."

At first Freekin had thought so, too, but since Steve's cousin in Minnesota had CSS, and he'd never met Freekin

in his life, it was impossible.

"No, sir, I'm not. I—"

"I know some doctors are calling it a vitamin deficiency, but I'm not buying it." Before Freekin could say anything, the principal sat behind his desk and got out a file. It was marked FRANKLIN RIPP. He opened it and reached for a large rubber stamp.

"If the team loses one game—*one*—you're out of here. And if I hear you asking a question—*one*—you're gone, no matter how much Karloff begs me. I hope we're clear."

"Yes, sir, we're clear," Freekin said.

"Very well." Principal Lugosi slammed the rubber stamp down hard on the page. It read: ON PROBATION.

"Get to class," he said with disgust.

Chapter Four:
In Which Lilly Stands by Her Man, and Pretty Makes a Chart

✳ ✳ ✳ ✳ ✳

He's back.

It was lunchtime in the school cafeteria. Lilly caught sight of Freekin in the reflection of the salad display case and frowned. She had heard that Principal Lugosi had readmitted him, but she hadn't seen him all morning. Not that she was looking for him.

His reflection stretched and grew. She caught him

checking his ears and heaved a wistful little sigh. For some reason, his ears fell off when he was around her. At first she had thought it was gross, but after a while, she had thought it was kind of . . . sweet.

She scowled and grabbed a salad. *Watch it, Lilly,* she told herself sternly. *You have moved on, to the Land of the Living. To the uncurious. He may have been declared innocent, but you know better.*

He was coming closer, and she debated getting out of the food line. But she was hungry; her doctor was on her case to eat more.

Besides, I can handle talking to him.

"Thank you," she told the lunch lady, who was handing her a plate heaped with Neapolitan Nacho Supreme, the latest Mystery Meat creation.

"Enjoy," the lunch lady said. "We're almost completely out of it."

Good, Lilly thought. *It tastes gross.*

"Hey, Lilly," Freekin said, coming up behind her.

She half-turned her head. "Oh, hi," she said, trying to sound polite but uninterested. "You're back."

"Yeah." He gazed at her with undisguised longing. "You look . . ." He blinked and looked down. "I mean, *that* looks . . . good." He pointed to her plate. "Mystery Meat. I thought you were a vegetarian."

She nodded. "I am. I mean, I was." She felt a sneeze coming on and fought against it. "My doctor wants me to get a lot of protein and build up my immune system so I won't catch Chronic Snickering Syndrome." She gave her head a little shake. "Not that I think it's you that's causing it," she added quickly. She knew that Steve's cousin in Minnesota had CSS.

"You're right. It's *not* me. And I don't think it's a vitamin deficiency, either," he added. "But I'm going to find out what does cause it."

Her eyes widened. "Freekin, no. You're in enough trouble," she said. At his dejected expression, she felt her heart breaking a little bit all over again. Just two weeks ago, they'd been so close to each other. She'd worked through her issues about him being undead and all. He'd come so far—getting on the football team, hanging with the jocks—and then he'd gone and ruined everything by asking all those horrible questions. She gave her head a little shake, trying to block out the nightmarish memories.

"Lilly, someone has to find out what's going on," he said.

"It doesn't have to be you." She felt her eyes well. She didn't want him to see how hard it was for her to talk to him. Didn't want him to hope that there was the slightest chance they could be together again. Because they couldn't. She had promised her parents and all the other cheerleaders that she would stay away from him.

And she had promised herself, too.

"I-I have to go," she said. But she couldn't exactly *go*. She had to stand in line to pay for her meal.

"It's okay, Lilly." He gave her a sad smile, then walked away.

She watched him go. The skateboarders welcomed him to their table. Steve glanced over at her and said something to Freekin. Freekin shook his head.

Lilly paid for her meal and headed for the cheerleading table.

"I can't believe he even had the nerve to talk to you," Deirdre muttered. "After everything he put you through."

"I know," Lily said softly as she picked up her fork. She eyed the Neapolitan Nacho Supreme, scooped up a healthy mouthful, and put it in her mouth. She chewed quietly and swallowed it down. She didn't like the taste, but she had promised her doctor she would eat it. The sooner she started, the sooner she'd be finished.

Just as she finished swallowing, she let out a big sneeze.

"Maybe it's like people say," Deirdre said. "Maybe

everybody's allergic to him and that's why people are getting Chronic Snickering Syndrome."

"That's not why," Lilly said, feeling the tiniest bit protective of Freekin.

Lilly, stop it, she told herself. *Freekin Ripp means nothing to you.* She sighed and ate another bite of Neapolitan Nacho Supreme.

While Freekin gathered his strength to make it to his next class, Pretty stared at the wall of Lilly in Freekin's room.

"Why Freekin love Lilly more?" It baffled her. Lilly was just a plain old human girl. But Pretty was pretty, if not beautiful. Her lip curled. Then she had a thought. Rolling over to Freekin's study desk, she pulled open a drawer and reached inside for his secret chart, folded up into squares and hidden beneath some other sheets of poster paper.

In big block letters, Freekin had written:

HOW TO BE MORE LIKE BRAD (SO I CAN GET LILLY BACK)

1. Coolness—band with Steve.

2. Buy presents—need money.

3. Looks—stop rotting.

4. Jock—make the football team.

There were check marks on numbers one, two, and

four. Freekin was still rotting, but he was *adorable*. Pretty wouldn't change a single piece of dead skin or one oozing lesion on him.

A light bulb went off. Pretty gnawed on her arm. She was so excited!

"Wowie zowie, Scary," she said. "Pretty makes chart! Pretty be more like Lilly!"

"*Gazeeka!*" Scary said, clapping his wings together.

"Then Pretty get her Freekin," she concluded. She set down his chart, dug in the drawer for another large piece of paper, grabbed a big fat purple highlighter, and got to work.

PRETTY SO MORE LIKE LILLY (PRETTY GET HER FREEKIN)

1. Girlie-girl makeover! (Fluttery eyeballs! Shiny mouth!)

2. Fashion! (One dress! Two! 1,213!)

3. ????

Pretty stared hard at her list. It was kind of short. She shrugged, chewed up the marker, and swallowed it down. Oh, well, it was a start!

"Great news. I can go back to school tomorrow," Brad told Lilly as he let her into his family's big fancy house. Lilly had come to visit him after cheerleading practice, as she had nearly every single day since he'd come down with Chronic Snickering Syndrome. She had faithfully

sat at his bedside while he sneezed like crazy and snorted like a donkey. It was terrifying, but she had done it.

"That's wonderful," she said.

"Yeah. I knew you'd be happy. Now we can go to the Nonspecific Winter Holiday Dance together."

Her heart skipped a beat as she smiled up at him. She had already bought her dress.

"Are you asking me to the dance?" she asked him.

"Of course I'm asking you." He winked at her and pointed at himself. "I'm the star quarterback." He pointed at her. "You're the head cheerleader. Plus we're the two best dancers in school. I think there's a law that says we have to go together."

"Well, I wouldn't want to break the law," she said. She flushed as an image of Freekin appeared in her mind.

"Me neither. I am totally law-abiding." He stretched and moved his shoulders. "The doctor wants me to get out of the house today for some fresh air and exercise. Let's go ice-skating."

"I'm in," Lilly said. But the truth was, she wasn't feeling all that great herself. She was a little afraid to tell anyone, and she wanted to be a supportive girlfriend, so she just smiled as they left the house and walked to Frozen Body Pond.

Lilly took a deep breath and blew it out again, watching the smokelike mist rise into the air in the winter wonderland of frosted tree branches and pure white snowdrifts. It had snowed that afternoon, and the ice on the pond was shiny and solid. Brad bundled her up in his letter jacket, and she ran her fingertips along the smooth satin lining. They rented skates and he bought her a pretzel and a cup of hot chocolate from a little cart.

"This tastes so good. All I could eat while I was sick was that awful gruel," he said as they skated side by side.

Lilly was so relieved—and happy, too, of course. Brad had been the first person in Snickering Willows to progress to the final stage of CSS—the chronic snickering. At first, the doctors thought he was laughing maniacally, and that he had gone crazy.

It was too bad about his dad, who really *had* gone crazy. Mr. Anderwater was locked away in the Snickering Willows Insane Asylum. There had been a fire at the Mystery Meat factory and something terrible had happened to him that night. Lilly wondered what was so horrible that it had driven him insane. Brad claimed he didn't know the details, and there was no way Lilly could delve deeper without asking questions.

She shuddered at the very thought.

"You look cold," Brad said.

She sneezed. Paling, she looked up at him. "I'm scared I'm going to catch CSS," she confessed.

"Even if you do, you'll survive. I did, and I'm almost over it," he reminded her.

"Shadesse is sicker than ever," she pointed out.

"Well, she's a goth," Brad said, as if that would explain it. "She got it from hanging out with *him*. That's how we all got it. I drank out of his water bottle in the locker room. Next thing I know, I'm in an ambulance."

She flushed. "I never ate or drank after *him*."

"Or kissed him . . ." Brad said. His voice was hard. His forehead was wrinkled.

"Or kissed him," she insisted. She remembered that she had been ready to kiss him, though. And *Freekin* had been the one to pull back at the last moment, and had given her a lecture about asking questions. Talk about ruining the mood!

"Promise me you'll *never* kiss him," Brad insisted.

Her heart skipped a beat.

"I . . . promise," she said, unsure if Brad noticed that she couldn't look him in the eye.

I. Am. Over. Freekin, she told herself. Over and over again.

Chapter Five:
In Which Pretty Gets Her Glam On!

✳ ✳ ✳

"Tra la la, la la la," Pretty sang as she and Scary headed for the mall.

She was going to get something called a makeover. And she was going to pay for it with her very own money. She and Scary had gathered up a sackful of coins from the fountain in the park. When people had extra, they just threw it in the water for other people to use.

"Pretty wants churros first," she told Scary. She loved churros.

"*Zibu*," Scary agreed. He wasn't as fond of the mall as Pretty was. To be honest, the mall was a little bit overwhelming for him. All the people, all the lights and noise! Scary was a bit too timid for the Land of the Living. He could be brave when he really had to be, but he was basically afraid of his own shadow.

They reached the big glass doors that slid open when Pretty trundled onto the rubber mat, and entered the magical kingdom of chrome, glass, and neon lights. But there had been some changes: fancy decorations of red and green. There were big green fuzzy circles of branches hanging on the sides of the escalators, and trees in storefront windows decorated with shiny stars and lights. And there was tinkling music. Pretty was enchanted. In the Underworld, it was dark all the time.

Gazing everywhere with all her eyes, she led the way to the escalator. Scary fluttered behind her, morphing into a big yellow balloon with a happy face on it.

The pair made a quick detour into the food court, where Pretty gobbled down five churros and Scary nibbled on one. She clutched her sack of money in her

sugary, sweaty palm and trundled into the department store. They wove their way around the glittering housewares displays.

There were more circles of branches and trees, and some moving statues of little creatures that looked like Underworlders. The creatures pretended to build toys beneath a banner that read SANTA'S ELVES MAKE DREAMS COME TRUE AT SNICKERING WILLOWS MALL. They wore pointed hats and their ears looked sharp enough to poke an eye out.

As the two friends passed through the home section of the store, Scary bobbed at the silverware pattern he'd picked out last time.

"Yes, yes, yes," Pretty said impatiently. "It so shiny. But Scary does not need."

Scary's happy face turned upside down. Pretty smiled secretly to herself. Scary's 1,300,006th birthday was coming up. She was planning to come back and buy him the silverware as a surprise.

Then they reached the makeup counter. Pretty thought back to the first time she had met Lilly. Her lip curled at the memory of all the cheerleaders laughing at her. She'd make them sorry. Not by eating their eyeballs, either. By decorating hers.

There was a lady at the counter with very tall hair, wearing a smock that read HIGHLY OVERPRICED PRODUCTS OF BEAUTÉ.

"Hiya," Pretty said, grabbing hold of one of the barstools at the counter and hoisting herself up. "Me wants—"

"Zelda!" the woman cried.

"No," Pretty said, shaking her head. "Me no Zelda. Me so Pretty!"

"Zelda, look!" The woman waved her hand at another lady with very red lips and big black glasses. "That couldn't be Anita's Peekapoo . . ."

"Why, yes, it is!" Zelda peered over the tops of her glasses. "My, she's gotten so big. Hello, doggie. She's a clever one, escaping from the groomers."

"I'd better take her back right away," said the lady with the tall hair. "She's too big to carry, though." She disappeared behind the counter, then came back up with a thick gold cord. "Here, this will do the trick."

She wrapped the cord around Pretty's neck.

"All right, doggie. Here, pup, pup, pup, come along now!" she sang, tugging on the cord. "Now, no need to be afraid of the groomers. They will make you look so cute!"

"Grrrr," Pretty growled, tugging at the cord. She thought very hard about throwing a fit. She could blow a thirty-foot spout of flame out of her mouth and all her eye sockets as well. She could yell so loudly, she would break every single piece of glass in the entire mall. She could rattle this human lady's bones until they were chewable little chunks.

She glanced up at Scary, who looked very anxious, and decided that was not the way to go. He'd be upset. Besides, Freekin could get in trouble, and he had just gotten *out* of trouble.

So for Freekin's sake, and Scary's, she let the lady drag her away from the makeup counter, down the escalator, and into a dog beauty shop called Fifi & Fidette, House of FrouFrou.

"Can't stay. Just bringing the dog back," the lady called, banging her painted fingertips on a silver bell as she tied Pretty's leash to the arm of a chair. She gave the bell another *ding-ding* and swept back out the door.

Before Pretty could figure out what to do, a voice called from the back.

"I'll be right there!"

Just in the nick of time, Scary changed into a little Welsh corgi.

"*Galeeka gazeebu,*" he whispered, wriggling his little body.

"You so sweetie," Pretty told him warmly. She took in his transformation. "You so cutie-pie."

"Oh, what adorable puppies!" cried a man with a kooky hairstyle as he approached the counter and saw them. He wore a bright pink apron with black doggie footprints on it, and a sparkly earring shaped like a doggie paw.

"Grrr," Pretty muttered, so very, very tired of being mistaken for a dog. It took all her strength to hold back from making a scene.

"Aren't you *darling!*" the man said, opening up a little gate, bending down, and petting her. He gave one of her ponytail ears a little squeeze. "You are a precious little princess!"

Okay, maybe not *all* her strength.

<hr>

Monsieur Scott-tay, the groomer at the dog beauty parlor, flea-bathed and clipped Pretty and Scary. He pampered and perfumed them. Then he put them in the drying booth while he gave a French poodle named Mademoiselle Poopee a French manicure.

The drying booth made them both itch. Pretty's tentacles started to lose their moist, slimy texture. With some regret for the anxiety it might cause Monsieur Scott-tay, Pretty chewed her way out of the booth and the two friends scurried out of the mall.

That certainly had not gone as she had planned!

As they bounded through the park, a high-pitched giggle suddenly assaulted Pretty's ears. She clenched her fists and covered her ears with a tentacle. She knew that laugh. She *hated* that laugh.

She trundled through a copse of trees and screeched to a halt. There she was, Yucky Lilly, sliding around on the ice with Bad Boy Brad. Brad was a mean, bad boy who had tried to hurt Freekin many times. Pretty knew it was a good thing that Lilly liked Brad. Human beings had rules about these things. If Lilly was with Brad, she was not allowed to be with Freekin. And that was exactly how Pretty wanted her—not with Freekin.

But just seeing Lilly made her blood boil. Too bad she couldn't just devour her. Maybe Pretty could breathe some fire and melt the ice they were sliding around on. If Brad and Lilly were good swimmers, maybe their heavy ice skates wouldn't drag them down to the frigid bottom of the pond.

Tra la la.

"*Woodiwoodi*," Scary begged. He didn't want her to cause a scene.

Pretty sighed. Scary hadn't changed back into his phantom shape, and Pretty suspected he liked his fancy new doggie look.

"Okie dokie," Pretty muttered. She bent over and scratched Scary behind the ears. She wondered what her kitties would think of him. "No melting. Pretty goes home. Scary goes home."

But instead of leaving, she took a step closer. Maybe if she pushed Lilly down . . . kind of forcefully . . .

No. Pretty had to behave.

The setting sun glinted off the ice. Pretty realized she could see herself in the shiny surface, and she bent down and stared with all seven of her eyes. She had cute little red polka-dot bows on her ponytail ears and a sparkling collar that looked just like a fancy necklace! She looked like one of those glittering trees!

"Oh, Scary, Pretty *likes* doggie makeover," she told Scary.

He wagged his tail and panted, *chuff-chuff-chuff-chuff-chuff.*

"Me so Pretty, pretty, pretty, pretty," she sang. She was far more beautiful than Yucky Lilly could ever hope to be.

Victorious, she and Scary walked through the streets of Snickering Willows. The Mystery Meat factory rose like a sinister castle against the graying sky. Billows of stinky, yellow-orange smoke puffed into the air.

The factory was a bad place. Pretty had seen something very weird going on in there. She just wasn't sure what it was. A bunch of people were sitting around a table, muttering about something in a can. When she'd tried to sneak down a ramp to listen harder, she'd accidentally rolled straight to the table. All the people had freaked out. So she'd set the place on fire to escape!

Then Bad Boy Brad's father chased her down 113 flights of stairs to the underground parking garage. He tried to shoot her! He told her if she ever told anyone what she had seen, he'd shoot them, too!

Then Pretty's kitties had stampeded to her rescue. They crawled over Brad's father until he was drowning in kitty fur and passed right out. Pretty took his car and zoomed it out of there.

Bad people, she thought, remembering the weird room with all the people talking in low voices. *Bad people with a secret. Bad, bad people.*

"*Woof*," Scary said, and giggled.

But what *was* it that she'd seen? Why were they all so worried?

She had never said a word about it to anyone, not

even Freekin. She didn't want to get him in trouble.

She shook off her musings as they neared Freekin's house. *La la la, on to more important things—Freekin!*

The light was on in his bedroom. Her heart beat a little faster. She hoped he was home to see how lovely she was!

Making sure Freekin's mommy, daddy, and doggie Sophie wouldn't see her, she climbed up the oak tree in his front yard and slithered across a branch into his room. Scary added a pair of wings to his corgi look and fluttered beside her.

Her kitties surrounded her and she gave them all smoochies. Then they sniffed and batted at Scary, who tumbled onto his back and stuck his stubby legs in the air, panting with joy.

The door opened. As Freekin had taught them, Pretty and Scary darted under the bed, away from the prying eyes of human beings. Pretty watched with all her eyes as the beloved shoes of Freekin walked into the room.

Freekin bent down and smiled at her and Scary. He was on a cell phone. Eagerly, she crawled back out. Then she twirled in a circle, showing off her red polka-dot bows and her sparkling collar.

"That's great," he said, and Pretty squealed with joy. He gave her a look that said, *Shh, I'm talking.*

With the phone pressed to his ear, he meandered over to his Wall of Lilly and stared up at the pictures. Pretty crawled up on his desk and swayed back and forth in front of them.

"Freekin," she whispered. "Look!"

But he turned sideways, as if he were avoiding her!

"Sorry, Raven, I couldn't hear you. Oh, man, tell her I said hi. If she can hear you over the snickering."

He hung up. "Shadesse is even worse," he told Pretty.

"Me so crying," she said. She gave her head a shake so he would see her bows.

He looked sad, too. Then his eyes widened and he smiled. The fungus on his front tooth caught the light. "Wow!" he said.

"Pretty!" she cried, fluttering all her eyelashes.

"Wow, Scary, you make a great dog." He walked right past Pretty, squatted down, and scratched Scary under his chin. "You even smell like a dog. Maybe you could play with Sophie sometime."

"Woof," Scary said shyly as he flopped over on his back again. His tail thumped against the floor.

Freekin patted Scary's doggie tummy and stood back up. Scary rolled over and got to his paws.

"Time for bed, guys. I'm going to go brush my teeth."

Pretty watched from her perch on his desk as he left the room. Her lip trembled. Her ears trembled. Her tentacles quivered with grief and despair. He hadn't even noticed her makeover! Hadn't seen her red bows, or her collar! What could she gnaw on? How could she *go* on?

Heartbroken, she crawled into her nest. She shut her eyes and pretended to be asleep, even though she was really waiting breathlessly for Freekin to come back and plant another kiss on her cheek.

But as luck would have it, she fell asleep, and so she didn't know if he had kissed her or not.

Chapter Six:
In Which Pretty's Plot Thickens!

The next morning, Freekin went downstairs for breakfast. His parents were smiling happily at each other. Sophie was lying under the table, whapping her tail on the floor in greeting.

"Good morning," Freekin said.

Mr. Ripp raised his coffee cup in Freekin's direction. "It is a good morning. I just got a call. I got the job! I'm

the new manager at Rigortoni's Pizza Parlor."

"Sweet, Dad! High-five!" He held his hand up and his dad slapped it. Their palms stuck together briefly, but his dad didn't seem to notice.

"I start today," his dad went on.

"That is so cool," Freekin said, relieved beyond the telling. He'd been afraid that no one would want to hire the father of the kid who got put on trial for asking questions.

"It's a great opportunity." Mr. Ripp smiled at Freekin. "I've got all kinds of plans. I'm going to talk to the Nonspecific Winter Holiday Dance committee about ordering our new pizza fingers for refreshments. Everybody loves Rigortoni's."

That was true. Rigortoni's was the best pizza parlor in Snickering Willows. Coach Karloff always ordered a stack of extra-large Mystery Meat-lovers pizzas for his post-game parties.

"Getting fired was the best thing that ever happened to me," Mr. Ripp went on. "I was never going to get promoted to the Ultra Top Secret Ingredients division. I was just going to rot in Top Secret. This is a chance to really do something with my life!"

I know the feeling, Freekin thought, pondering his own next move.

Sitting on Freekin's bed, Pretty swung her tentacles, nibbled daintily on one of Sophie's old chew toys, and studied her list.

PRETTY SO MORE LIKE LILLY (PRETTY GET HER FREEKIN)

1. Girlie-girl makeover! (Fluttery eyeballs! Shiny mouth!)

2. Fashion! (One dress! Two! 1,213!)

3. ????

She was about to suggest another trip to the mall to look for item number two when Freekin's door opened. Grabbing her chart, she dove under the bed in case Freekin had brought company. Still wriggling around in his corgi disguise, Scary scooted in after her.

Freekin and three Good Boys walked into the room. They were Steve, Raven, and the other pale boy, the friendly one, Tuberculosis. Still, Good Boys or not, she and Scary stayed under the bed.

"Let's get down to business," Freekin said. From her vantage point, Pretty watched his adorable shoes walk across the room. As quietly as she could, she smoothed her crinkled chart and settled in to listen.

Freekin looked at each of his friends in turn—Steve, Raven, and Tuberculosis. Were they really up for this?

They would have to defy more than a century of tradition to help him. Could they handle it?

"Okay, guys, listen," he said. "You know what's coming. Asking questions."

"Very well," Tuberculosis said, although his voice was a little shaky.

"I'm already a believer," Steve reminded them all. "If Freekin hadn't asked some tough questions, I probably would have died skateboarding on Daredevil Bridge."

"Let's make a list of our questions and answers," Freekin told the three. He got out a big piece of paper and a marker.

The Cause and Cure of Chronic Snickering Syndrome, Freekin wrote.

"What do we know?" Freekin asked, tapping the paper with the tip of the marker. There it was, question number one, asked aloud and proud. To their credit, his friends stayed calm.

"We know the symptoms," Steve said. "First your nose starts to itch and then it gets red. You sneeze a lot. Some people get rashes on their foreheads. Then it all gets worse." He swallowed hard. "Then you start to snicker."

"Like a donkey," Raven added.

"You can't eat anything," Tuberculosis put in.

"Only gruel," Raven murmured. "That's all Shadesse can stomach."

"Some people have the cold symptoms for a long time," Freekin said, scribbling down all the symptoms:

Itchy red swollen nose

Sneezing

Snickering

Steve half-raised his hand. "People in Snickering Willows started getting CSS around the time that you got back."

Freekin wrote on his piece of paper:

I came back.

"Principal Lugosi said I brought it with me," Freekin said. "I thought he was right, until you told me that your cousin in Minnesota had it, too."

"Brandon." Steve thought a moment. "We sent Brandon some presents for his birthday. Maybe there's a clue there."

"Perhaps something you sent Brandon causes CSS," Raven ventured. He took a deep breath and swallowed hard. "What were the gifts?"

"Wow, you asked a question, Raven," Freekin said. "How do you feel?"

Raven wiped his forehead. "Thus far, I have not felt the need to vomit," he replied. "Although I do think

I had better sit down." He lowered himself carefully onto Freekin's bed. Tuberculosis gave him a pat on the shoulder.

"You are the king," Tuberculosis murmured, awed.

"We gave Brandon a jar of Snickering Willows Puckering Pickles and a T-shirt from Snickering Willows Cards and Gifts," Steve replied.

"That's a weird combination," Freekin said.

Steve shrugged. "He's a weird cousin."

Freekin wrote:

Presents for Brandon: Pickles. T-shirt.

"Perhaps it is pickles that carry the Chronic Snickering Syndrome," Raven suggested. "Or T-shirts, or something else in the gift shop."

"My mom bought an extra jar of pickles," Steve said, scratching his somewhat swollen, red-tinted nose. "I had a couple of them last night, and it looks like I'm getting CSS."

"It does indeed," Raven said sympathetically.

"Your nose is huge," Tuberculosis concurred.

"So are you saying that everyone who has CSS got it from eating pickles?" Freekin asked. "Or wearing T-shirts? Or going into the gift shop?"

Tuberculosis looked a little faint. "So many questions," he murmured.

"Steady." Now it was Raven's turn to pat his shoulder. "I believe that after a time, it will not seem so horrible."

"We could ask people if they've been eating pickles," Freekin said. He heard himself. "I mean, we could *find out* if they've been eating pickles." They shouldn't ask questions in public. The problem was, once you got in the habit of asking questions, it was difficult not to.

Freekin wrote:

Pickle-eaters, T-shirt wearers, gift-shop shoppers.

"I'll try to find out if any of the other guys on the football team have had any contact with pickles or T-shirts, or have gone in the gift shop," Freekin said.

"Cool." Steve nodded. "I'll check out the other skateboarders."

"We shall survey the goths," Raven said, including Tuberculosis.

"My family owns Snickering Willows Foodatorium," Tuberculosis said. "It's possible we sell those pickles. I can provide samples if we need any."

"Okay." Freekin capped his marker. "I think this is a good start. If we work together, we can solve this mystery."

Mystery? Pretty thought as she lay beneath Freekin's bed. She had been listening to every single word her wonderful boy had spoken. *Work together?*

Maybe that was how to get Freekin's attention. She could help him solve this mystery! Yes! Her mind raced. Her eyes spun. She gave Scary a tight squeeze and he wagged his corgi tail.

"Nice doggie," she told him. He panted and rolled over on his back. As she scratched his tummy, she started making plans for item number three on her list.

3. *Pretty helps her Freekin.*

Ha! What had Yucky Lilly ever done for him?

———— ✳ ✳ ✳ ✳ ————

The next morning, Freekin was one of the first to arrive at football practice. Coach Karloff gave him a nod and put a check mark by his name on the roster. It was the first time Freekin had seen the coach since his house arrest. The coach had been out with CSS, and he looked alarmingly thin.

"Hey, Ripp," he said. "Glad to see your brush with the law is over." He raised his brows. "And you're done with . . ." He lowered his voice. ". . . the question-asking."

"Yes, coach," Freekin lied. He cleared his throat. "So. Puckering Pickles," he began. "Very tasty." He waited for a response. But the coach had returned his attention to his clipboard.

Freekin started warming up, doing jumping jacks and running in place. In the next few minutes, most of his teammates joined him—Vernia, Sontgerath, Greenfield—each one giving him a smile and a wave. It was still so amazing to him that he was a football player. That probably wouldn't have happened if he hadn't died.

"So, guys," he said, not even huffing as they exercised. He never ran out of breath because he never had to breathe. "Puckering Pickles." That was all he had to say. Not, "Do you like them?" Since no one in Snickering Willows grew up asking questions, everyone knew how to follow the seemingly random statements people made in place of asking questions.

Some of the players told Freekin that they loved Puckering Pickles. Others did not love them. But he couldn't find a pattern between those who had probably eaten pickles and those who had suffered from Chronic Snickering Syndrome. In fact, half the team was still out sick, and all he could get out of Coach Karloff was that for the last week, he himself had eaten nothing but gruel. That was why he was so thin.

Brad Anderwater also mentioned that he had eaten nothing but gruel for a week, and Freekin began to wonder if perhaps gruel helped to cure CSS. He decided to add that to his chart when he got home.

On the subject of T-shirts, he got absolutely nowhere.

Tra la la.

Pretty, on the other hand, was on fire. She knew about the Horatio Snickering III Municipal Library because she and Scary had gone there once with Freekin. Freekin had done some research for a report on the Trojan War. She knew about books and she even knew how to read. And she remembered that there was a section that would help Freekin: the mystery section!

Before they entered the library, Scary reluctantly abandoned his corgi shape because no dogs were allowed. He became a hooded sweatshirt, which Pretty wore into the library so that *she* wouldn't be thrown out for being a dog.

The first thing they saw when they entered the building was a huge oil painting of a man in baggy pants, a vest, and a coat. He was holding a pocket watch. A brass sign beneath the painting read, HORATIO SNICKERING III, OUR BELOVED FOUNDER. She had seen him before. There were pictures and statues of him everywhere. There was even a statue identical to this very portrait in the park, beside a fountain filled with money.

"Hiya," Pretty whispered, grinning with excitement.

Together they trundled over to the mystery section and Pretty grabbed as many books as she could carry.

Then, when she placed them on the checkout counter, she nearly fell right over from shock!

The librarian at the counter had been on Freekin's jury. She was the old lady who had held her nose when Freekin had walked into the courtroom. She was a mean, Bad Lady!

Pretty had to work very hard not to growl or have a fit.

"I need your library card," the old woman demanded.

Pretty stared at her. She was stumped. She didn't remember anything about a library card. Maybe she had been off playing when Freekin gave the Bad Lady his own library card. Pretty wanted to ask what a library card was, but she knew she couldn't ask any questions. So she drummed her tentacles on the floor while she pondered what to do.

"*Zeekeeweekee,*" Scary whispered in her ear. Aha! *He* remembered seeing Freekin's library card!

"Me come back soon," Pretty told the old lady.

"I'll only hold these books here for fifteen minutes," the woman replied.

Pretty and Scary darted behind the nearest bookcase. Proud to be of service, Scary immediately transformed into a small white card with FRANKLIN RIPP, BELOVED SON written on it.

"*Galawaganeekee*," he announced.

"You so smarty-pants," Pretty said approvingly. She trundled back to the old lady and handed her the "library card." The lady ran Scary over some kind of scanner and handed Pretty her immense tower of books without so much as looking at her. Which was a good thing, since Pretty was standing there without her Scary sweatshirt disguise. The old lady probably would have assumed she was a dog and thrown her out on her bottom.

"These are due back in two weeks," the Bad Lady said.

"Okie-dokie," Pretty replied.

Pretty escaped with her treasures. Scary flew them into Freekin's room while Pretty crawled in on her own. Once she got comfy in her nest beneath Freekin's bed, Scary turned into a flashlight.

Eagerly, Pretty flipped open the first book and began to read with her two big eyes about a great detective named Sherlock Holmes. She used her five little eyes to read a second book, about a gecko detective.

After five hours and six books, Pretty narrowed all seven of her eyes. There was definitely a common thread emerging. In a mystery, death meant crime.

Tapping her tentacles against the floor, she mentally reviewed the very weird visit she'd taken to the Mystery

Meat factory a few weeks prior. When Bad Boy Brad's father laid eyes on her, he had tried to kill her, and he told her he would kill anyone she told about what she had seen there.

"Scary," she said slowly, tapping a page in the book about Sherlock Holmes. "Elementary-my-dear-Watson visits crime scene. Clues. Investigations. Mystery Meat factory is crime scene?"

She read through some of her books again, clacking her fangs as she puzzled it through.

Finally she slammed her books shut and nodded. "Pretty goes to factory," she informed him. "Scary goes to factory. Sneaky-peeky."

"*Woodiwoodi,*" Scary protested.

Pretty trundled into Freekin's closet. As her darling cats batted at her tentacles, she dug around until she found a black jacket. On her, it became a trench coat that reached the floor. That was good. Detectives wore trench coats. Then she located a hat. Detectives wore hats. This one said SNICKERING WILLOWS LITTLE SAPLINGS BASEBALL LEAGUE.

Perfect!

Suitably attired, she went over to the window. As her kitties meowed in protest, she slithered out. Scary fluttered nervously behind her.

"Heigh-ho," she told Scary. "Scary takes Pretty there."

"*Zibu*," Scary said very reluctantly as he turned into a flying carpet and floated beside the tree branch. Pretty plopped from the branch onto the carpet and Scary rose into the sky. Once they had gained some altitude, he changed into a helicopter.

"Too noisy," she advised him. "Pretty so sneaky."

He changed into a supersecret spy plane. Pretty cheered and clapped her hands. "Scary so sneaky!"

Then she took the controls.

"Heigh-ho, Scary!" she cried, such a beautiful creature and mystery-solver extraordinaire! "Me so Pretty!"

BATCH 1314
(TOASTY TWINKLE)

Chapter Seven:
In Which Pretty Boldly Goes!

Snow pellets dropped from the sky like flakes of dead skin as Scary flew Pretty to the Snickering Willows Mystery Meat factory. The moon was a large gangrenous pustule. The sight made Pretty a tiny bit homesick for the Underworld, where, while there was no moon, there was plenty of gangrene.

She could smell the factory's spewing smoke well

before they reached the compound itself. It was stinky. The bricks were smudged with soot, and some of the windows were cracked. It was not a nice place.

On her previous visit to the factory, all the bad things had happened on the 113th floor, so Pretty told Scary to hover there while she tried to peer into a very tiny, grimy window. She couldn't see a thing. They'd have to go up in the elevator, like the first time they'd snuck in.

So they flew into the underground parking garage, where Pretty's kitties had stampeded Brad Anderwater's father. No kitties today. No Mr. Anderwater, either.

Scary changed back into himself and the two hopped into the first elevator they saw. The door slid shut. Pretty looked for the button for the 113th floor, but there were no buttons at all. *None.* She panicked. Something was not right! Before she could tell Scary to get back out, it rose.

"Uh-oh, Scary," she said. "Elevator prison!"

"*Woodiwoodi.*" Scary put his wings around her shoulders and hid his face against the back of her neck.

After a few seconds, the doors opened, facing an upright sign in a metal stand that read ULTRA TOP SECRET PROCESSING DIVISION. She had no idea what that meant. She frowned at the sign. Should she investigate further? What would Sherlock do?

Then the elevator made a loud beep, startling her, and she jumped out of the elevator. Scary fluttered out, his eyes as big as hamburgers, and hovered beside her shoulder. Seeing nothing amiss, she was about to jump back in and go downstairs when the door shut. There was no button on the wall to open it back up.

"Hmmm," Pretty said, crossing her arms and tapping one of her tentacles, trying to decide what to do. Then she heard footsteps padding down the hall to the left. Someone was coming! They had to hide!

Anxiously, she grabbed Scary and scooted around the sign. They zoomed into a long passageway behind it. Pretty kept looking over her shoulder as they barreled along.

Then she heard the elevator beep again! *Aieee!* She ran faster.

Just as quickly, she slammed on the brakes.

At the end of the passageway, a silver-haired man in a white coat and a hard hat stood with his back to them. He placed his palm in the center of a glowing yellow rectangle positioned in the upper half of a stainless steel door. A handprint shape glowed green beneath his hand and the door swung open.

The man crossed the threshold. Revving her tentacles so fast they whirred, Pretty raced to the door and dragged Scary through with her before it closed.

They reached an intersection, with corridors branching off to the left and the right. About ten feet beyond, the man stopped walking and half-turned his head. Oh no! Had he heard them?

Pretty looked for a place to hide. Against the wall of the intersection to her right, she spotted several metal shelves loaded with brown cardboard boxes. They were all labeled BATCH 1313 (NEAPOLITAN NACHO). Pretty grabbed Scary and yanked open the first box she could reach. She threw Scary in and dove in after him.

She landed on something hard and round. Pressing her hand over Scary's mouth, she held her breath and waited. The man's footsteps grew fainter and fainter. Then she could hear nothing.

"Pretty wants light," she said.

Scary turned into a flashlight. Pretty shined him on the hard, round object.

It was a human skull. When she and Scary had thrown a welcome home party for Freekin, they had dug up lots of skulls from the graveyard to decorate his room. That was the first time they had discovered an empty grave.

"Maybe Pretty having party today. Maybe Scary having party today. Happy birthday, welcome home, get well soon," she whispered as she picked up the skull and made it talk to Scary. There was a tag tied to the jaw. She read it. SB, AUGUST 31. Something about those letters and date was familiar, but Pretty couldn't place it.

She showed it to Scary. "Scary knows this? Special letters? Special day?" she asked.

Scary shrugged his wings and shook his head.

"Investigation. Pretty finds clue," she mused. She wished she had brought a notebook and a pen. "Pretty on case!"

Setting down the skull, she peeked out of the box and listened hard. Hearing nothing, she pushed up the lid and crawled out. Scary followed her.

She waited. Her heart was pounding. She took a breath and peeked into the box next to the one in which they had hidden.

There was another skull!

"Wowie zowie, Scary," she whispered, intrigued.

Then she thought she heard rustling just beyond the shelf. Gesturing for Scary to follow her, she tiptoed back the way they had come and peeked around the corner. She thought again about retreating to the elevator.

There was more rustling. "Eek," Pretty whispered,

and jumped back into the main corridor. To her left, she heard the stainless steel door open. Someone was coming! Their path back to the elevator was blocked. The safest route—which was not very safe at all—was to continue down the main corridor, the way the silver-haired man had gone.

That was the way she went, Scary flying above her, whimpering anxiously.

Pretty reminded herself that although she was frightened, she was not defenseless. And she was motivated. She was doing this for Freekin. She was doing this so he would see how devoted she was to him. Yucky Lilly was just a silly cheerleader. But she, Pretty, was using her little gray cells to help him save Snickering Willows!

Oh no! At the end of the hall, there was *another* door. She glanced back over her shoulder, trying to decide if they should go through it.

"*Woodiwoodi*," Scary whispered.

"Pretty is here," she assured him.

Very cautiously, she pushed on the door and poked her head around it.

On the other side, shelves reached from floor to ceiling, crammed with boxes labeled BATCH 1314 (TOASTY TWINKLE).

"Okay, Ed, let's snap it up," someone said.

"Uh-oh, Scary," Pretty said, clutching him.

Scary immediately turned into a box labeled BATCH 1314 (TOASTY TWINKLE), and Pretty hopped inside.

There were more footsteps. They grew louder and louder.

"On my way, Dr. Lao," said another voice, very close.

Suddenly they were being lifted into the air! Someone had picked them up!

Pretty cringed inside Scary. "Scary sees what?" she whispered as softly as she could.

They stopped moving. Then the Scary-box rose higher in the air as someone shook it back and forth. She heard Scary whimper very, very quietly. The box was lowered, and there was scratching along the lid, like fingernails. Then she saw the pink tips of someone's fingers prying it open!

She tried to make herself smaller, but she was no shape-shifting phantom. However, she *was* a fire-spewing monster, and she could cause a scene if she and Scary got in trouble. She had set the Mystery Meat factory on fire once, and she would do it again if she had to. Taking a deep breath, she prepared herself for extra-super-hot flame throwing.

"Ed!" the other voice shouted impatiently.

Pretty's eyes began to spin. Steam rose from the top of her head.

The fingers disappeared. The lid closed.

Pretty sagged as she shut down her fire-breathing system. Close call.

On she bobbed. She wondered if Scary knew what was happening. The suspense was killing her. Her fangs began to clack. Sinking them into her arm, she clenched her free hand into a fist so she wouldn't try to peek. If the man who was carrying Scary saw eyeballs, he would definitely stop and investigate.

Off in the distance, she heard strange metallic sounds, like rattling chains and squeaky wheels. The sounds got louder and squeakier. Steam hissed.

Machines, Pretty thought.

There was more rattling. Then a sort of *chunka-chunka-chunka*.

Big machines.

Next, something roared like a very angry monster. It was so loud, the box vibrated.

Enormous machines!

Pretty whimpered again, a little more loudly, and Scary trembled all around her. With an unsteady hand, Pretty patted the floor of the box and mouthed, "Scary so safe. Pretty so safe."

With a *whump*, Scary was suddenly set down, one end resting much higher than the other. Pretty slid to the other side of the box in a jumble of eyeballs and tentacles.

"Scary?" she whispered.

Clank-clank-clank. Hissss. ROAR!

"Scary?" she called more loudly.

The noises grew bigger, scarier. The Scary-box got shakier and tiltier, sending Pretty rolling onto her stomach.

"*Gabibu wazee!*" Scary told her above the roar.

So she gathered her tentacles beneath herself, lifted the lid, and peeked out. Gah! It smelled horrible! Worse than rotten eggs mixed with monkey poo!

Her eyes teared from the terrible odor. She blinked them clear and saw that she and Scary were on a conveyer belt, creeping slowly along in a long parade of other boxes identical to Scary. The line was moving on an incline, past a crisscrossing spiderweb of copper pipes and metal gears that tick-tick-ticked in slow clockwise circles. The conveyer belt stretched out forever, moving upward at an angle like an escalator at the mall, only turning right, left, right again, as it headed for higher ground.

"*Woodiwoodi woodiwoodi woodiwoodi,*" Scary said, terrified.

"Pretty spits fire," she reminded him, giving him a reassuring pat. "Pretty saves Scary."

"This ought to do it," a voice boomed out above her. She lowered the lid just a smidge, so that she was better concealed but could still see out. The silver-haired man in the lab coat and hard hat was walking beside the conveyer belt, marking things on a clipboard. A second man was following close behind him. He was dressed in a plaid shirt and a pair of jeans. "By next Monday morning, we'll have eliminated the problem."

"But Dr. Lao, I think this just might be adding to the problem." Pretty recognized the voice of Ed, the man who had put them onto the conveyer belt. "We had to resort to SB August 31 and the others because we weren't getting enough raw material the old way. No one's asking questions anymore, so no one gets sent away."

"No one was asking questions until that Ripp kid came back from the dead," Dr. Lao replied. Pretty heard the loathing in his voice, and she gnawed a little harder on her arm. "And according to what we've been hearing, he's been asking all the *wrong* questions. He's big trouble."

All seven of Pretty's eyes widened. They were talking about Freekin!

"I can't believe the judge declared a mistrial." Ed

shook his head. "If Ripp had been sent away, we wouldn't be in this mess."

"You're wrong, Ed," Dr. Lao replied. "Curiosity is highly contagious, which is why our great founder outlawed it. It's true that it would be good for production if our citizens would ask harmless questions, like they did in the old days. People got arrested in droves for asking, 'How are you? Do you think it will rain?' But all that's been bred out of Snickering Willowites."

Paling, Ed made gagging noises as he grabbed his stomach and hunched over. "Dr. Lao, please," he begged. "I-I can't handle that kind of language."

"Sorry, Ed," Dr. Lao said, not sounding sorry at all. "But you see my point. People *aren't* asking those kinds of innocent little questions." He held his clipboard against his chest. "We don't know if Ian Anderwater got rid of that weird little talking dog thing that snuck into our meeting! But we *do* know that that's when Ripp started asking questions."

And now they were talking about Pretty! *She* was the "talking dog thing" that had snuck into their meeting.

"I see your point," Ed said, wiping his forehead. "I really need this job. I have a family to feed."

"So we'll make this batch of Toasty Twinkle to calm the town down. I'm optimistic that it will work very well." He smiled at Ed, but his eyes were cold and mean. "We're going to test it on Ian Anderwater tonight."

"Interesting . . ." Ed began. "He is, after all, locked up now . . ."

Dr. Lao nodded. "Yes. Up until now, people have written off what he's been saying as the ravings of a madman. But with the increase in the Curiosity level of the population, it's possible someone might really listen to him. Maybe even Ripp. We can't take the chance that anyone will make the connection between Neapolitan Nacho and CSS. So we have to muzzle Anderwater."

Pretty frowned. *What? Connection is what? Anderwater has muzzle? Anderwater is dog?*

"Right, sir," Ed said. "And then we'll see what happens next. After we've made the batch of Toasty Twinkle and distributed it to the town . . ."

"Exactly," Dr. Lao said ominously. "Maybe we'll make another batch. Maybe we'll figure out how to make something else to control—I mean, benefit—our good citizens." He patted Ed on the back. "Science marches on, Ed. Science marches on."

The men kept walking. Pretty's eyes spun; she was agog at what she'd heard. *Trouble, big trouble! Pretty must help!*

She gnawed, her mind racing as she and Scary bobbed along. Then they turned a sharp left and their speed picked

up. Heat plumed against Pretty's skin as she was thrown backward onto her bottom.

Clank-clank-clank-clank-hiss-hiss-ROAR!

"Scary," she whispered. "Noise is what? Show Pretty! Pretty sees!"

"*Woodiwoodiwoodiwoodi.*"

Scary reshaped himself, creating a little view screen in the front part of the box.

Aieee! What Pretty saw curled her tentacles. They were mere inches away from the tippity-top of the incline. Dead center at its peak, a huge chomping machine hung over the conveyer belt, its eager, hungry mouth lined with dozens of gleaming, serrated teeth. It was twenty Prettys tall and six Prettys wide, and razor-sharp teeth gleamed as its upper jaw smashed down on the next box, hard enough to crush a human being. Something gray oozed out of the box. It smelled terrible. It smelled rotten.

The machine swallowed the shreds of the box and the gray ooze, and they were gone. It ate the next box. More gray stuff spewed out. It was just as stinky.

"*Woodiwoodi,*" Scary said again.

"Once this basic material has been compressed into little chunks of Mystery Meat, we'll glitterize it with Toasty Twinkle just before we package it. That way, it will be at maximum strength when it's delivered to

Snickering Willows School for lunch," Dr. Lao said. "Just the way we processed Neapolitan Nacho. According to my timetable, glitterization should take place around six o'clock Monday morning."

"In the Ultra Top Secret Enhancement Laboratory," Ed said.

"Correct. Our team will have to wear hazardous materials suits."

"Already issued, sir," Ed informed him.

"Excellent. Since the Toasty Twinkle solution is so highly concentrated, the batch will be quite small. People only need to eat a tiny amount for it to have its desired effect."

During their conversation, the Scary-box scudded ever closer to the chomper. Pretty had a problem. She could set everything on fire to save herself and Scary, but she didn't want these Bad Men to know she had heard every word they had uttered. Plus she needed to know more—like if they were planning to hurt Freekin. But now she and Scary were only three boxes away from the cruncher.

Make that two!

"Oh, oh," she moaned, thumping her tentacles.

Then, in her anxiety, she bit down so hard on her own arm that she screamed.

"AIEEEEEEE!" she shrieked, leaping up out of the Scary-box like a jack-in-the box.

Dr. Lao and Ed screamed, too. Startled out of his wits, Scary changed back to his own Scary self and threw his wings around Pretty, yelling at the top of his little phantom lungs.

"It's the dog! Catch it!" Dr. Lao shouted.

Pretty shrieked again. Her eyes spun like pinwheels.

Neither man moved. They just kept screaming.

Scary yelled.

Pretty's eyes spun faster and faster. Her fangs clacked.

And then the most amazing thing happened: The men's eyes rolled back in their heads, and they collapsed onto the floor.

Wowie zowie! Pretty had no idea what had just happened, but she had no time to think about it.

"Heigh-ho, Scary!" she cried. She grabbed his wing with her hand. Together they leaped off the conveyer belt and darted back the way they had come, back through the room filled with boxes of Ultra Top Secret Ingredients for BATCH 1314 (TOASTY TWINKLE), and up the main corridor to the stainless steel door.

Pretty took a deep breath and pushed on the door. It didn't open. She was about to chew it open when Scary

reshaped himself flat as a leaf and disappeared beneath the door. The door hummed opened, revealing that Scary had assumed the shape of a human hand. The rectangle on the door was glowing green.

"Scary so awesome!" she congratulated him. He beamed and changed back into himself.

Half expecting an alarm to sound, she tip-tentacled across the threshold. Next came the big sign, and then the corridor. They were standing mere feet away from the elevator door. But there was still no button, no way to summon it.

"Yoo-hoo, knock-knock," she whispered anxiously under her breath. Scary nervously fluttered his wings.

Maybe there was another way out. She thought about her first visit to the factory. When she had started the fire, she had not been able to take the elevator to the parking garage. But she'd still gone back down, by taking the . . .

"Scary! Stairs!" she cried.

Seeing no stairway door next to the elevator, she grabbed Scary by the wing and hung a right, searching for a door farther down the corridor. Sure enough, ten feet beyond, there was a door marked STAIRS.

"Yee-ha!" she cried, pushing it open.

Beautiful concrete stairs awaited her intrepid

tentacles. Together they flew safely down to ground level. Then Scary turned himself back into the flying carpet, and Pretty rode him down to the underground parking garage. There Scary morphed once more, this time into the supersecret spy plane, and they booked it out of there.

"Whew, Scary! Close call!" she cried.

"*Zibu*," he agreed.

"Zoom home," she ordered him. "Freekin in danger! Pretty saves her Freekin!"

Chapter Eight:
In Which Tragedy Strikes!

————✳—✳—————

Pretty and Scary soared through the sky and blasted home to Freekin's house as fast as they could go.

"Freekin!" Pretty whispered loudly as her kitties converged, eagerly greeting her. "Freekin, knock-knock! Come out, come out, wherever you are!"

She looked under his bed and in his closet. Next she scuttled across the hall and looked in the bathroom. His daddy was watching TV, and he didn't notice when she crept past him. His mommy was in the kitchen—*yum, sugar cookies!*—but he wasn't there. He wasn't in the garage or out back, either.

"Now what, Scary?" she demanded. She tapped her tentacles as she paced the bedroom floor. She paged through some of her mystery books.

Lightbulb! She tried IMing all his friends.

FREEKIN: Knock-knock, U R home?

She tried calling their phone numbers.

"At the tone, please record your message."

"Hiya," she said in a low, gravelly Freekin voice. "Hiya, dude, 'sup, dog. Woof woof. Me so Freekin in da house. Me say hi, call back."

No one picked up. No one called back.

She and Scary paced the room. Her kitties trotted around her, meowing for attention. Should she go to Freekin's mommy and daddy? Would they be able to listen to a single word she said, or would they just start screaming and get out the chain saws?

"Pretty does what? Scary does what?" she muttered. She gnawed on her arm, then on Sophie's chew toy, then on the leg of Freekin's bed. Scary flew around the room, nervous and fluttery as a trapped bird. He loved his Freekin, too.

"*Ian Anderwater*," Scary said suddenly. "*Aleekiliezi*." He morphed into an arrow and pointed at Freekin's desktop computer.

"Good idea, Scary!" Pretty cried, and typed "Ian Anderwater" into a search engine. "Looky, looky, looky! Snickering Willows Insane Asylum," she read off to Scary. She had no idea what that meant. She typed that in, too. It was a place! A place for crazy human beings! And Ian Anderwater was in room number 217!

"Tra la la," she sang excitedly, typing in perfect rhythm to the clacking of her teeth as she searched for directions.

Bongo bingo! Street names! Maps! She printed them out. Scary peered over her shoulder and nodded.

Scary transformed back into his supersecret spy plane shape. Pretty leaped to the controls and they flew through the brain-colored snow and pus-colored moonlight.

At last they came to a dark and eerie silhouette cut out against the sky. Lights flickered wildly in its windows, and its arched front door resembled a frown.

"Go down," Pretty told Scary. She pointed to the snow-covered roof. "Go there, Scary."

"*Zibu*," he said, descending. They landed on the roof. Pretty hopped out and he changed back into his little phantom self, hovering beside her.

"*Woodiwoodi*," he whispered.

"Pretty so careful," she promised him. She took his wing and they shuffled through the snow until she found a door and pushed it open. Then she and Scary peered down a steep flight of stairs.

"Sweatshirt," she whispered. Scary became her hooded sweatshirt and sat on her head. She started down the stairs, which let out in a dark, dim corridor. The wood paneling in the hallway smelled dusty and old. On the wall, a sign said ROOMS 200–220.

She consulted her computer printout. She needed room 217.

As quietly as she could, she crept down the hall. Scary clung tightly to her head. To her right, someone cried like a baby. To her left, someone laughed like a polymorphous thundergorilla, scourge of the Underworld. And farther down the hall, someone was doing both.

"It's all gone! Gone! No one will ever know! No one!" cried a man's voice.

And it was coming from room 217.

Taking a deep breath, Pretty reached up and pushed open the door. It was very dark, but a stream of moonlight revealed a struggling man dressed in a pair of pajamas with his back against the window. Two other men stood on either side of him, each holding one of his arms. One

was very tall, with dark eyebrows and a sour face. The other one was short and skinny, and his smile gave Pretty the willies.

"I won't talk, I swear I won't," the man in the bathrobe said. "Just make sure there are no cats! No cats!"

"He's crazy," the tall man said. "No one is going to listen to him."

"Dr. Lao sent us here to make sure of that," the skinny man said as he reached into his pocket. Pretty tensed and trundled toward them. No one noticed her.

"Bad batch! Thirteen-thirteen!" Ian Anderwater shouted. "SB August 31! Mistake! Kill the talking dog!"

The skinny man pulled his hand out of his pocket. He was holding a syringe. The tall man pushed Ian Anderwater's pajama sleeve up.

"Quick," he told the skinny man.

"Twinkle, twinkle, little star," the skinny man sang to Mr. Anderwater. Then, before Pretty could do a thing, he plunged the needle into Mr. Anderwater's arm.

"No cats!" Mr. Anderwater yelled. Then his knees buckled and his eyelids flickered. "Missssss . . . take . . . thirrrrrrrrrrrrteeeeeeeen . . ."

He slumped forward, and would have fallen to the floor, if the two men hadn't kept him upright.

"Let's get him back into bed," the tall man said.

At a sign from Pretty, Scary flew under the bed. Pretty crawled in after him, panting as she lay on her stomach, peering out.

The two men were dragging Ian Anderwater away from the window.

"If Toasty Twinkle works the way Dr. Lao says it does, he won't be any more trouble," the skinny man said.

The two men walked out of the room and shut the door. Pretty scooted back from under the bed and bobbed up beside Ian Anderwater.

"Brad's daddy?" she whispered, shaking his shoulder. "Knock-knock?" He didn't respond.

She glanced back at the door. She had to follow those Bad Men. She had to see what else they were going to do.

"Scary stays here," she ordered him.

"*Woodiwoodi*," he said nervously.

"Scary so brave," Pretty said.

He fluttered beside the unconscious man and gave her a brave thumbs-up as she flung herself across the room and opened the door.

* * *

This is Belle. The title of this chapter is freaking me out. What tragedy? Is someone going to die? You should just say. This isn't fair.

My dear Belle, these questions are music to my ears! They are proof to me that I've still got the old narrative magic. You may be asking them as well, Dear Reader. Surely it has occurred to you that although Freekin is undead, bad things can still happen to him. If, for example, he can't kiss Lilly, he will be leaving Snickering Willows soon.

What about Pretty? The sweet little creature is over a million years old. But is she immortal?

What about Scary? If he is an ancient phantom, why is he afraid of his own shadow? There must be reasons why he is so timid.

Perhaps Sophie is in danger. She was quite ill, until Pretty resuscitated her. And we have grown to love Freekin's friends and family, have we not?

I wish I could blurt out the answers to all these questions. But such is not the way of professional Narrators. We have all taken an oath to keep you on the edge of your seat for as long as possible, and as you may recall, I am trying to prove to the International Order of Narrators that I can be trusted in matters such as these.

And so, we must leave Pretty as she chases after the Bad Men, and turn our attention to Freekin, who has been noticeably absent from these pages for some time. At the time of the events in this chapter, he was at Coach

Karloff's house for a very special occasion. Gilberto Gonzalez, the famed football star, had returned to his hometown of Snickering Willows for a visit, and he had agreed to watch the Friday night game. The Snickering Willows Carnivores had totally creamed the Mocking Maples Decimators, and Freekin had been declared MVP again.

The cheerleaders were invited, too, and they were trickling in. Lilly had yet to show.

Gil was sitting around shooting the breeze when the big delivery of Rigortoni's pizzas arrived from the restaurant. Freekin smiled, wondering if his father had made any of the pizzas himself.

"Help yourself, boys," said the coach's wife, Mrs. Karloff, as the guys swarmed the pizza table.

"I'm looking for Neapolitan Nacho," Brian Vernia said, experimentally lifting a pizza box lid.

Mrs. Karloff shook her head. "They took it off the menu."

There was a chorus of groans and protests.

"No way." Brian wrinkled his forehead. "That's the best flavor they ever had. I ate tons of it before I got sick. The whole time I was lying in bed, I was dreaming about eating it again. Now I'm all better and it's gone."

Wait a minute, Freekin thought. He froze, dumbstruck. *Could it be?*

"Brian, you ate tons of Neapolitan Nacho . . . and you got Chronic Snickering Syndrome," he said slowly.

"Couldn't get enough." Brian reached into the closest Mystery Meat-lovers box and grabbed up two slices, slapping them onto a paper plate. "I even ate it for breakfast."

Freekin blinked. His mind raced. He started making a mental list:

1. The school cafeteria introduced Neapolitan Nacho Supreme on the first day of school.

2. Kids started getting sick.

3. Other people in the community got sick—even Sophie, my dog.

4. And I snuck her all my Neapolitan Nacho, because I don't need to eat.

5. Lilly has been eating it like crazy recently.

Where was Lilly? He wondered if she was staying away because he was there. But Brad kept watching the door, too, as if he was expecting her any minute.

Then Coach Karloff ambled over with Gonzalez in tow. "Ripp," he said. He smiled at Gonzalez. "Now you can see what I've been talking about."

"Those plays were quite amazing," Gonzalez said. "I was most impressed when your quarterback faked out the Decimators by pretending your head was the ball."

"Thanks," Freekin said. Actually, that hadn't been the original play. Brad had torn off his head out of spite, not strategy. He claimed it was an accident, but Freekin knew better.

"And I am guessing it does not hurt you when they pull you apart . . ." Gonzalez lifted his eyebrows and looked pointedly at Freekin. Freekin shook his head. "*Dios mio*, I almost wish I were undead," Gonzalez said.

"Thanks," Freekin replied. He hesitated. "Coach, about Neapolitan Nacho . . ."

"Yeah, too bad about the pizza," Coach Karloff said. "I swear, I love that stuff. That was the worst part about being sick. All I could keep down was gruel." He patted his stomach. "Lost a few pounds, so that was good."

He clapped Gonzalez on the shoulder. "Let me introduce you to Brad Anderwater. He's the quarterback you're talking about."

Coach Karloff and Gonzalez sauntered over to Brad. Brad's eyes widened and he pumped Gonzalez's arm. He looked like a six-year-old who had just met Santa Claus.

Then, with a gust of cold air, the front door opened and Deirdre hurried into the warm house. She had her cell phone up against her ear and her face was pinched with concern.

"Okay, Lilly, feel better," she said. She clicked her phone shut as Molly and Janeece, two of the other cheerleaders, swirled around her.

"Lilly's not coming," she told the girls. "She sounds awful. I'm supposed to find Brad and let him know." She pointed toward the other side of the room. "There he is."

"I hope she doesn't have *it*." Janeece lowered her voice.

"She didn't say," Deirdre replied, chewing her lower lip, "but she was sneezing a lot." She headed for Brad.

"Oh, no," Molly and Janeece said in unison, as they trailed behind Deirdre.

"Hey, Deirdre," Freekin said, stepping into her path.

She gave Freekin a hard look. "Hi, Freekin. Excuse me. I have to go talk to Lilly's boyfriend."

Her phone rang again.

"Hello," she said. "Oh, hi, Mrs. Weezbrock. Lilly . . ." Her mouth dropped open. She looked up from the phone at the girls. "Lilly's being taken to Horatio Snickering III Memorial Hospital! She's got Chronic Snickering Syndrome!"

Janeece and Molly screamed.

Without a moment's hesitation, Freekin scooted around Deirdre and raced for the door.

Chapter Nine:
In Which Tragedy Snickers!

Lilly's in the hospital!

Freekin dashed out to the street and looked for a taxi. The snow was falling heavily, making it difficult to see. Cars blew past, but he didn't see any cabs. He was just about to go back into the house and ask someone for a ride when a big yellow cab pulled to the curb.

"Horatio Snickering III Memorial Hospital, and step on it," Freekin told the cabbie. He felt in his jeans pocket for some cash.

Poor Lilly. If anything happens to her . . .

"Go faster," Freekin said as the cab streaked down the streets.

"Kid, it's snowing," the cabbie protested.

It seemed to take forever for the cab to reach the hospital. Freekin dropped a wad of cash in the man's outstretched hand and darted inside.

He ran up to the reception desk. A woman in a pink-and-white-striped hat and matching jumper glanced up from a computer screen.

"Good evening," she said. She looked him up and down. "The morgue is in the basement."

"I'm looking for Lilly Weezbrock."

"Let me see . . ." The woman typed in Lilly's name. Her eyes widened. "*Oh.*" She cleared her throat. "She's been taken to the super-contagious ward. I'm afraid no one can see her. There's a waiting room on her floor. Her parents are in there now."

"Okay, thanks," he said.

"Floor thirteen," she said. "The elevators are down that hall."

"Thank you." He raced past her and jumped into the nearest elevator. There was a crowd inside, and it seemed the elevator stopped at every single floor. He thought he would burst apart by the time it arrived at the thirteenth floor. He flew out and stopped in the hallway.

An arrow pointed to the left. WAITING ROOM.

He went to the right instead, ducking his head into each and every room. He was undead. He couldn't catch *anything*. Except maybe a football. He smelled disinfectant and flowers. Super-contagious old man, super-contagious old lady, super-contagious little girl . . . where was Lilly?

Just then, two nurses wearing masks came out of the last room on the left. There was a loud sneeze.

And then, horribly . . . a snicker. And another. And a third, so loud it echoed down the hall.

The taller nurse sadly shook her head. "Such a pretty girl. What a shame."

"A lot of people get over it," the other one replied.

"But some don't," the first nurse said. "Her parents are about to lose their minds."

They looked at each other and sighed. They went

on down the corridor, their shoes squeaking on the tile floor.

As soon as Freekin was sure the coast was clear, he darted into the room. His ears tingled, and he touched each of them in turn to make sure he'd glued them on tight.

Dressed in a pale blue hospital gown, Lilly lay snickering in the bed. Her nose was as big as a doorknob, and as red as a flaming charcoal briquette. Her cheeks were wet with tears.

"Lilly," Freekin said, rushing to her bedside. "I came as soon as I heard. Your mom called Deirdre at the party."

"Oh, Freekin," she said, but it came out "Dreekin." She snickered. "I'm so scared."

"I'm here, Lilly," he said. His ears were getting hot.

She sneezed again. And then she snickered. Sneezed. Snickered.

"Maybe you heard the doctors tell my parents about how I'm doing." That was the Snickering Willows way of asking if he had seen her parents, and if he knew how sick she was.

Her cheeks reddened and she looked down at her

hands. "Maybe someone else was in there, too."

That was her way of asking if Brad had shown up.

"I didn't go to the waiting room," he said. "I came straight here."

"*Ohsnrkkkrrrrr*," she replied, as twin tears rolled down her cheeks. Freekin pulled some tissues from a box beside her bed and handed them to her. "Thank you."

As she dabbed her face, she sneezed. "I'm . . . I'm sorry, Freekin. Maybe if I listened to you, maybe if I could have made myself ask why this was happening in Snnnnickerrrrrring Willows . . ." She snickered. "My world's been turned upside down!"

She started crying.

"Lilly," he said. "Listen, I think I know what causes this." And then he realized that he didn't know that at all. Steve's cousin Brandon had CSS, and as far as Freekin knew, he hadn't eaten any Neapolitan Nacho Mystery Meat.

Darn it!

"Okay. What?" She caught her breath. "Freekin, *I asked a question!*" She looked even more frightened as she clapped her hands across her mouth.

"It's okay, Lilly. You just told me that you need to

ask questions, remember?" His mind was racing. He had to talk to Steve right away. And Shadesse. Maybe she held the key to the puzzle.

She swallowed hard and played with her tissue, sneezing a few times. "You're . . . right." She caught her breath. "Actually, it's kind of . . . *exciting*."

"Good, Lilly. That's good." He nodded and leaned toward her. He glanced at the door and lowered his voice to a whisper.

"I'm going to find a cure for CSS. I promise you."

Lilly gazed at him with her big blue bloodshot eyes, and then she snickered very, very hard. She looked down at the tissue, wadded it in her fist, and inhaled deeply. Her breath came out in a series of quick snickers.

"Thank you." She took another deep breath. "Um, you were at Coach Karloff's house. I guess other people were there, too*snickkrrrr* . . ."

He could see how badly she wanted to see Brad, and it hurt. But that didn't matter right now. How he felt didn't matter. Lilly mattered.

"Brad was at Coach's house," he told her. "I'm sure he'll be here soon."

"Sure." She snickered again. "But *you're* here *now*."

He didn't know what to say. He could tell that she was confused, and he was enthralled. His ears were practically break-dancing, and he touched them again to make sure they were still attached to his head.

She snickered and snorted. Then her features softened as she gazed at him the way she used to, before she had walked out of his unlife. "I'm sorry I doubted you."

"Oh, it's okay, Lilly," he murmured. "I understand. I'm just an undead guy with a bad case of Curiosity."

"I don't think you do understand," she said. And very, very shyly, she let her fingers brush against his hand.

His eyes widened. His ears jittered. Was she trying to get back together with him? Did he dare ask her that? What if he asked, and she was so repulsed she told him to leave?

I have to be with her to be able to kiss her. And I have to kiss her to stay in the Land of the Living, he thought. *But more than that, I have to kiss her because that's my dream.*

And yet, he was still too afraid to ask that all-important question: Will you be my girlfriend? It was so ironic: He had no fear of asking questions that could get him thrown out of town, but he couldn't ask

the question that would bring him and Lilly together.

"I have to go now," he told her. "I'll check back and see how you are."

"Okay*snicckerrr*," she said.

He blasted out the door to the sounds of her snickering.

<hr>

After injecting Mr. Anderwater, the two Bad Men had jumped into a long black car and driven away from the insane asylum. Realizing there was no way she could chase after them, Pretty raced back into Mr. Anderwater's room and summoned Scary. He changed into the super-secret spy plane and they took to the skies. After half an hour of searching, they gave up. So they returned to the insane asylum, to check on Mr. Anderwater.

To their surprise, he was walking down the corridor fully dressed. His gait was wooden and his face was slack. Pretty ducked behind Scary, who transformed into a potted plant. After all, Mr. Anderwater had tried to kill her before. He'd been ordered to get rid of the "talking dog" who had bumbled into the top secret meeting on the 113th floor.

"Everything is fine now," Mr. Anderwater said, to no one in particular. "There are no problems. Everything is wonderful."

"Scary," she said, blinking. She was bewildered. "Pretty needs her Freekin!"

An hour after Freekin left Lilly's room, Brad showed up. He was wearing what looked to be a gas mask. It was big and green and covered half his face. Lilly was snickering like a donkey by then, and her stomach was cramping and sore. She had a headache to boot.

"Lilly, I came as soon as Deirdre told me you were in here," Brad said, keeping his distance from the bed. He sounded like Darth Vader.

"Oh, you must have . . ." *Snicker.* ". . . been at Coach Karloff's . . ." *Snicker snicker.* ". . . party."

"Yes. Gilberto Gonzalez wanted to talk to me, but I left. To be with you."

"Huh." She narrowed her eyes as she fought to suppress her next snickering fit. It was hard to hold a conversation. "That's interesting *snicksnicksnickrrrr.* Freekin heard about it at the party, too. And he left here an hour*snicker* ago."

Brad's mouth dropped open. "Freekin. Came. Here."

Sneeze, snicker. Sneeze, snicker snicker snicker snicker. "Yes. He. Did."

"I-I had to get a ride," Brad said, averting his gaze. "That's why it took me a little while longer." He walked a little closer to her bed, but not very much. "I would have gotten here sooner, but I wanted to buy you some flowers. The stores were all closed. I thought about picking some flowers out of the hospital garden, but—"

He was lying to her. Lilly was shocked—not only that he would lie to her, but also because he expected her to be so charmed by him that she'd believe whatever nonsense he told her.

"Brad, come on, it's the middle . . ." *Snicker.* ". . . of winter*snicksnicksnick*. There are no flowers in the hospital garden." *Snickersnickersnicker.* "Tell me the truth. You came after the party was over." *Snicker.* "You had your fun, and *then* you came to see me."

Snickerrrrrrrrrr.

"No." He shook his head. "I don't know what that stupid dead loser told you—"

"Freekin is not dead. He is undead, and what we said to each other*snicksnicksnickerrrrrrrr* is *snicksnicksnick* none of your business," she said angrily. *Snicker.* "But this is what *I'm* telling *you*: I'm not your girlfriend anymore."

She wasn't sure her words registered. He just

stared at her, his eyes bulging above his gas mask. Then he vigorously shook his head.

"You . . . you don't mean that, Lilly," he breathed. "You're sick. You have a fever. We're still going to the Nonspecific Winter Holiday Dance—"

Lilly looked away from him and toward the wall. She snickered so hard, tears came to her eyes. "I am sick," she agreed. "And we might still be going to the dance—but not with each other. Now go away!"

Snicker snicker snicker snicker!

"Young man, there is no reason for you to be in here! No one is allowed to visit this patient," said a voice from the door. Lilly recognized it as one of the nurses. "She's highly contagious, and I doubt that mask will do you any good at all. Leave at once or I'll inform security."

"Okay, okay," Brad snapped. "Lilly, this isn't over," he called to her. "That *thing* is not coming between us!"

"Leave *now*!" the nurse ordered him.

"I'm going, Lilly, but I am not gone!" Brad shouted.

Then his footsteps stomped away.

"Go away and stay away," Lilly murmured. Then . . . horribly . . . she began to snicker nonstop.

Snickersnickersnickersnickersnickersnickersnicker snickersnickersnickersnickersnickersnickersnicker snickersnickersnickersnickersnickersnickersnicker snickersnickersnickersnickersnickersnickersnicker . . .

"Code orange!" the nurse shouted. "Emergency! I need help stat!"

Help me, Freekin, Lilly thought. *Please!*

------ ✳ ✳ ✳ ✳ ------

It was a lucky thing that Horatio Snickering III Memorial Hospital was close to Freekin's house, since he had no money for another cab. There might have been some more wadded-up bills in his letter jacket, but he had left it at Coach Karloff's house. He didn't need it; since he was undead, he didn't get cold.

Lilly, he thought, seeing her lying helplessly in her hospital bed. Remembering how she had brushed her fingers against his. *Why* hadn't he asked her if she wanted to get back together?

For the same reason he hadn't kissed her six months ago, the day before he had died:

"Because you're stupid," he chided himself.

Chapter Ten:
In Which Our Heroes from the Afterlife Join Forces!

FREEKIN: Steve, R U SURE all U sent Brandon was pickles & a T-shirt?

SK8BOARDER STEVE: Yes.

FREEKIN: R U totally sure?

SK8BOARDER STEVE: I'll go ask Mom. BRB

Freekin drummed his fingers on his desk. There was a noise at his window, and Pretty and Scary tumbled in to the room.

"Freekin, run!" Pretty shrieked. She threw her arms around him. Her tentacles pounded against the floor so hard that she sent them both spinning in a circle. "Bad men! Toasty Twinkle! Bad batch! Connection! Run!"

"Pretty, what's the matter?" he demanded, fighting to keep his balance. Then Scary changed into a suitcase and flopped himself open on Freekin's bed.

"Woodiwoodigazeee," he pleaded, stretching out a wing and shooting it into the top drawer of Freekin's dresser. He grabbed Freekin's pajamas and tossed them into the Scary-suitcase. Next he reached for Freekin's guitar and threw that in, too.

"Wait! Stop! What are you doing?"

Pretty started babbling in a foreign language. Her eyes spun like plates on sticks. And as he stared at them, the hair on the back of his neck rose. His flesh crawled. His stomach lurched. Fear dropped over him like a net, making him tremble and shake.

"P-p-p-p-retty, stop," he said in a hoarse gasp.

Then his IM chimed, indicating Steve's return. The sound distracted Pretty, and she turned her head toward the computer. Still babbling, she raced over to it and pressed her seven eyes up against the monitor.

"Good Boy," she announced. "Good Boy Steve."

As Freekin gingerly moved her aside, his fear began

to fade. What on earth had she done to him? He wasn't sure she had meant to do anything. She didn't seem to realize something had just happened.

SK8BOARDER STEVE: F, my mom put a can of Neapolitan Nacho in Brandon's package! Last minute addition, didn't tell me B4!

"Bingo!" Freekin cried. He threw his arms around Pretty and lifted her toward the ceiling. "Pretty, I think Neapolitan Nacho is making people sick!"

"Toasty Twinkle, Freekin!" she replied. "Please, please!"

In her jumbled Pretty way, she told him about her sleuthing at the factory and the insane asylum.

"So Mr. Anderwater kept saying it was all gone," Freekin said, when she was finished. "And that there were bad ingredients. And then after they gave him that shot, he turned into a zombie!"

"Yes, yes, yes, yes, yes!" she screamed. "Twinkle-twinkle-twinkle! Zombie!"

Freekin bent down on one knee, coming eye level with Pretty. "Pretty, Scary, you guys followed me from the Underworld. You're my two best friends. Will you help me figure out what's going on?"

Freekin asks Pretty to help! Freekin so loves Pretty! Pretty so loves Freekin!

"Tra-la-la! Pretty helps her Freekin, Pretty helps her Freekin." The she kissed him all over his face so hard, she actually took an ear off.

"*Woodiwoodiwoodiwoodiwoodi,*" Scary-as-suitcase fretted on the bed.

Pretty's eyes widened. "Scary says run," Pretty translated. "Maybe Scary so smart?"

"I can't run," Freekin told her. "I have to stay here and fix this."

She blinked her seven eyes at him. "Pretty says why? Why you?"

"Because." He thought a moment. It was the most important question anyone had ever asked him. Why him? Why Franklin "Freekin" Ripp, and not someone else? Why not a real hero?

Because . . . he knew what happened when people didn't ask the right questions, and no one else did. Because people in this town would rather die than ask a question, but they didn't know what he knew. They didn't know what it was like to leave things behind. To leave . . . people . . . behind.

"Because I should," he told her.

"Oooooh," Pretty breathed, fluttering her lashes. She held onto his knee even more tightly and bounced up and down on her tentacles. "Freekin so hero!"

He pulled her ponytail ear. "Naw. I'm just a regular kid. Well, just a regular undead kid."

She waggled her head back and forth. "No, no. You so hero," she insisted.

"So you'll help me?" he asked her.

"Yes! I do!" she cried.

"Zibu," Scary added. He popped back into his phantom shape, leaving Freekin's pajamas and guitar on the bed.

"Thanks, guys. You're my best friends," Freekin told them both. "Okay, we need a plan." He reached for the drawer where he kept his lists.

Pretty earnestly clutched his knee. "Pretty goes to crime scene! Freekin goes to crime scene! Scary goes to crime scene! *Now!*"

———— ✳ ✳ ✳ ————

At Pretty's insistence, Freekin put on dark clothes and a hat so he would look "sneakier." Then the three friends set out for the boiling smokestacks and puffing chimneys of the Snickering Willows Mystery Meat factory.

Scary flew them into the parking garage, which was filled to the brim with cars. Strangely, there were a lot of people working the Friday night shift.

Pretty located the stairs to the Ultra Top Secret Ingredients processing area. Scary made himself thin enough to slide under the door with the yellow rectangle.

Then he opened the door from the other side. No alarm sounded. Nothing happened. They were in.

"Pretty shows her Freekin," Pretty said, grabbing Freekin's hand and dragging him along the passageway. They came to an intersection and Pretty guided Freekin to the right. A bunch of shelves stood against the wall. On it were approximately twelve boxes. They were labeled BATCH 1314 (TOASTY TWINKLE).

"No, no, no!" Pretty said under her breath. "Batch 1313 is where? Neapolitan Nacho is where?" She trundled over to a box and opened it. Inside lay an inch-long plastic vial of what looked like gold glitter. Freekin held it up to the light. It shimmered and shone.

"What is this stuff?" he asked aloud. He looked left, then right, and hid it in his pants pocket.

"Pretty finds more," she announced, lifting the lid off the next box. Meanwhile, Scary flew over to a third box and disappeared inside it. He popped back out with a vial identical to the ones Freekin and Pretty were holding.

"Give them to me," Freekin said.

He was stashing them in his jacket pockets when voices sounded in the corridor. His eyes widened. *Now* what should they do?

"Aieee, Freekin," Pretty said. She picked him up bodily—she was very strong—and tried to stuff him into one of the boxes. There was no way he would fit.

"So Anderwater's been taken care of," said a man's deep voice. By the sound of it, the man was nearly at the intersection. He would see Pretty, Freekin, and Scary in a matter of seconds!

"Yes, sir," said a second man.

"Woodiwoodi," Scary said. Then he changed into a little wheeled trash can.

"Good!" Freekin told him.

"Courthouse," Pretty whispered. "Sneaky-sneaky." She reached up her hands. "Freekin helps Pretty?"

As he bent down and picked her up, Scary lifted his lid. Freekin set her carefully inside.

"You, there," the owner of the voice said to Freekin as Freekin closed the lid. "What are you doing?" He had curly black hair and he was wearing a white lab coat over a business suit. The other man was blond.

He asked me a question, Freekin thought. Freekin lowered his head so the man wouldn't see his face. No one else in Snickering Willows looked like Freekin. "Just taking out the trash, sir."

"Very well," said the black-haired man.

Freekin moved past them and headed for the door.

"What's the status on Dr. Lao and Ed Wood?" the dark-haired man continued.

"Both are still in a coma," the blond answered. "We're baffled."

"Well, if it was caused by Toasty Twinkle, those are even better results than we anticipated," the dark-haired man observed.

Freekin wheeled Scary as slowly as he dared, listening to every word. Comas? What were these Mystery Meat guys up to? They were mad scientists!

He reached the door. He wondered if he was supposed to have some kind of key or access code to get it open. With those two men in the hall, Scary couldn't transform from his trash-can shape to slide underneath and open it from the other side.

"Pretty, help me," he whispered.

"Uh-oh," Pretty whispered back. "Pretty makes scene?"

Then *fwommm*, the door opened. With an air of urgent self-importance, a man and a woman, also in lab coats, crossed the threshold. The man held the door open for Freekin, who wheeled his trash can through.

"Wow, that was close," Freekin said as they hurried back toward the stairs. As soon as he pushed through that door, Scary morphed into a flying carpet. Pretty climbed on and gestured for Freekin to do the same.

"Zoom!" she cried, and Scary flew them down the

flights of stairs to the underground parking garage. Then he became a supersecret spy plane and raced them out of there. Pretty sat at the controls and she was a highly skilled pilot, loop-di-looping into the sky above the very, very busy Snickering Willows Mystery Meat factory.

"Wow!" Freekin cried, holding on tight to his seat in the cockpit. "Is this what you guys do while I'm at school?"

Pretty gave him a wide grin. "We so elementary, my dear!" she cried.

"These guys are planning something big. I want to go to the hospital and check on Lilly," he said.

Pretty raised her brows. "Lilly in hospital?"

"Yes. She's got Chronic Snickering Syndrome. It's horrible," he said. "I'm so glad you guys are helping me. I've got to figure out what's going on before she gets any worse."

Pretty swallowed hard. "Me so helping," she said in a tiny voice.

Pretty, Freekin, and Scary reached Snickering Willows General Hospital in no time. Scary flew outside the building and hovered beside the window to Lilly's room. Freekin and Pretty balanced on the ledge while Pretty pulled it open with her superstrength. Freekin crept in first. Pretty scooted in after him. The moonlight gleamed into the otherwise darkened room.

"Lilly?" Freekin whispered, as he tiptoed toward her bed. It was empty!

"Oh, no," Freekin murmured. "She couldn't have . . ."

He couldn't say the word he was thinking, but *I* can, since I am your Narrator. It is "died." Consider for a moment the chaos that would erupt in Freekin's life if Lilly were dead. What would that mean? What would happen? Imagine the possibilities! It makes your head spin, doesn't it?

This is Belle. Jumping Josephina, just get to the point. Did she die or not?

Then Freekin spotted a chart lying on the nightstand of the empty bed. He grabbed it and ran back to the window, toward the moonlight.

Discharged. Patient's condition improved.

He was so relieved, he had to sit down on the bed before he fell down on the floor. "Maybe people get better if they stop eating Neapolitan Nacho," he said. "But then what about Shadesse—why is she still sick if all she's eating is gruel?" Freekin scratched his head and accidentally pulled out a clump of hair. "Let's keep moving."

"Freekin goes where? Pretty goes where?" Pretty asked eagerly.

He frowned at her. "To see Lilly, of course."

Then Pretty said something he couldn't quite hear.

✳ ✳ ✳ ✳

So off they flew to Lilly's one-story brick house. After Scary deposited him on her lawn, Freekin told Pretty and Scary to wait for him at the curb. He tapped softly against Lilly's window until the drapes opened and there she was! She was wearing a bathrobe and her hair was kind of loose and glowing in the moonlight. She looked beautiful.

"Lilly," Freekin breathed. "I was so worried about you."

She smiled, but it was a very strange, stiff smile. "I'm fine, Freekin," she said. Her voice was very flat. "Just fine." She yawned. "I want to go back to bed."

He frowned. "Lilly? Are you *fine* fine?"

"Fine," she said again. "Just tired."

"Lilly," he said, reaching for her. But she closed the drapes.

He frowned. Either she had changed her mind about how she felt about him, or something was very, very wrong. Toasty Twinkle wrong.

✳ ✳ ✳ ✳

As Scary perched on her shoulder, Pretty watched Freekin from the curb. Her heart was very anxious, but she kept her tears in check. *She* was so helping, not Yucky Lilly. Surely Freekin would finally realize that Pretty was his one true love!

"Hiya," she said, smiling brightly as Freekin loped up beside her.

"Man, I'm glad you're here," he told her. "This thing's way too big for me to handle on my own. I think they gave Lilly Toasty Twinkle at the hospital. She's still awake, but it's like she's a robot. It's terrible."

"Me so here," she assured him. "Me so sneaky, me so brave."

"Yes. You're all that and more," he replied, tugging on her ponytail ear.

Giggling, she spun in a circle and threw herself against his knees. "Me so Pretty," she said softly.

He took her hand. "Let's go. We have a lot to do."

He took her hand!

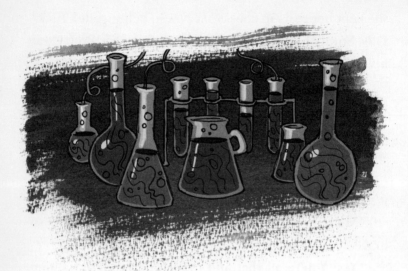

Chapter Eleven:
In Which Pretty Plus
Freekin Equals...?

FREEKIN: Howz Shadesse?

DEATHBEPROUD: Worse. The doctors are stymied. No one can help.

FREEKIN: I'm almost positive it's Neapolitan Nacho.

DEATHBEPROUD: But she eats only gruel. Her mother has confirmed this.

FREEKIN: ☹ I went to Mystery Meat factory, got a

sample of new flavor. Toasty Twinkle. They're going to use it on us on Monday. Makes us zombies. But I think it cured Lilly of CSS extra-fast.

DEATHBEPROUD: ?! I cannot get away. Parents are home, we are playing Disease Scrabble. Tuberculosis is a star chemistry student. He is surely up, working on his science fair project. Here is his e-mail address: incurableromantic@sw.com. We give Toasty Twinkle to Shadesse?

FREEKIN: After we get the cure? Possible!

DEATHBEPROUD: That would be tremendous. I have come to care for Shadesse a great deal.

Wow, Raven has a crush on someone, Freekin thought. He quickly e-mailed Tuberculosis, who IMed him at once and told him to come over right away. Of course Tuberculosis was up late. He was a goth.

Scary flew Freekin and Pretty to a turreted house in the middle of a forested section of town. It was a creepy-cool goth-type house. When Pretty saw it, she clapped her hands.

"Castle!" she cried.

Scary landed behind some bushes. As Tuberculosis had instructed, Freekin and Pretty went down a flight of stairs and knocked at the door to the basement.

"Okay, here it is. We need to find out what's in it,"

Freekin told Tuberculosis, handing him the three vials of golden glittery stuff. The goth lived in the basement of his parents' house, and he had a miniature chemistry laboratory set up on one side of his bedroom. "Apparently they're going to spray it on some Mystery Meat at six A.M. on Monday."

"Very well," Tuberculosis said. He ticked his glance at Pretty, and color splashed his pale cheeks. "I haven't seen you around lately." He gestured to her jumper. "I like your dead bunny head."

Pretty preened as she and Freekin followed Tuberculosis across the room to his microscope. Tuberculosis sprinkled some of the glitter on a slide and placed it beneath the microscope. Freekin and Pretty watched while he twirled the knob.

"Hmmm," Tuberculosis said. "Guar gum, polysorbate 60, arsenocarcinohydroxide . . . and something that's moving around. Something living. But I don't know what it is . . ." He scratched his forehead. "I've got some books in the other room . . ."

He left the slide under the microscope and disappeared through a door.

"Tuberculosis likes fashion," Pretty told Freekin, holding out the hem of her dress and turning this way and that. "Pretty chart, item number two."

Freekin chuckled, not completely understanding what she was saying. But when did he?

"He still thinks you're my hot little sister. You two better watch it, or I'll get jealous."

Pretty giggled uncontrollably. Freekin put his finger to his lips to remind her to be a little quiet. Still giggling, she trundled over to the microscope and peered through the viewer with one of her big eyes, then the other one, then one of her little eyes. She caught her breath.

"Virus," she whispered to Freekin. "Tell Tuberculosis virus."

"What?" he whispered back at her. "What are you talking about?"

She smiled at him proudly. "Me reading books, books, books. Mystery books. Library. *The Case of the Vicious Virus. Forensics for Morons.*" She pointed at the slide. "Virus."

Tuberculosis came back into the room with an open book in his hands. "There's nothing in here that looks like these things. They're little wriggling Zs."

"Could it be . . . a virus?" Freekin asked as casually as he could.

Tuberculosis stopped walking. "I hadn't thought of that." He looked into the viewer again. "Yes! It *is* a virus. Good work, Freekin! That's amazing biological detective work." He almost smiled, but since he was a goth, he didn't quite. "Let me go get another book."

And so it went on for hours, with Pretty guiding Tuberculosis's research from afar. They worked through the night. Freekin went home to make an appearance for Sunday breakfast while Pretty rummaged through her tower of library books for anything that might help them.

Then he checked in with Raven.

DEATHBEPROUD: Dark traveler, you are a genius! I texted Shadesse, and I have learned that Shadesse's mother flavored her gruel with Neapolitan Nacho! She has run out of it and there is no more to buy! There is hope!

FREEKIN: ☺! Rock! So glad! Going back to T's house now.

DEATHBEPROUD: I wish you luck, walker of the shadows.

When Scary returned Pretty and Freekin to Tuberculosis's house, the goth greeted them at the basement door in a black apron and protective goggles. He was carrying a bubbling beaker of blue liquid with a pair of tongs.

"I've got it," he announced. "*It's Apatheticus Majoris.*"

"Good! What's that?" Freekin asked, as Pretty turned her back and silently clapped her hands together in victory.

"Rows of Z-shaped viruses that makes *zzzzz* chains. It makes people apathetic," Tuberculosis explained. "And . . ." He frowned. "It's only found in the human body, Freekin. They must have figured out a way to manufacture it, unless they're extracting it from donors or something. Hmmm . . ." His voice dropped and he mumbled to himself as he paged through one of Pretty's helpful books. He yawned long and hard.

"Oh, no! You have it!" Freekin cried. "*Apatheticus Majoris!* Now all we have to do is find the antidote!"

"Freekin, I am not apathetic. I am only tired. I need to rest," Tuberculosis said apologetically. "I've been up all weekend."

By then, it was nearly ten o'clock on Sunday night. When you were undead and never needed to sleep, it was easy to lose track of time.

Freekin made a face. "Pretty said . . . I mean, I heard that they're planning to spray this stuff on the batch of Toasty Twinkle Mystery Meat at six o'clock tomorrow morning. They're going to serve it at lunch tomorrow at school."

Freekin clapped his forehead as he imagined the chain of events. "Then after everyone eats it, no one will care about what went wrong with Neapolitan Nacho. No one will care about anything! They're going to turn us into zombies! That must be why they're doing it!"

"I'll keep working on it," Tuberculosis said. "But I have got to lie down for a couple of hours. I can't think straight anymore."

"Fine. We should go anyway—before my parents realize I'm not home. IM me when you wake up."

"I will," Tuberculosis promised. "Be careful going home," he said, walking Freekin and Pretty to the basement door. He gave Pretty a little wink. "Take care."

"Pretty takes care," she said, blushing. "Takes care of Freekin!"

Pretty, Freekin, and Scary flew home in the super-secret spy plane. They soared above the town, which was hunkering down for the night. Black and ominous against the moon, the Mystery Meat factory pumped fumes of smoke and steam into the air. Seated beside Pretty in the cockpit, Freekin watched it with a deep sense of foreboding . . . and purpose.

"We have to stop them, Pretty," Freekin said. "Together."

"Pretty stops them," she said. Grinning, she stuck her hand down the front of her jumper and pulled out one of the vials of glittering Toasty Twinkle. "Freekin stops them. Pretty so mad scientist! Freekin so mad scientist!"

"Wow, Pretty, you're amazing," Freekin said. "I would never have guessed you were so clever!"

"Me so clever. Me so sweet," she told him, pushing down on the stick. The Scary plane spiraled toward Freekin's roof. Then Scary *poofed* into two open parachutes attached to the backs of Freekin and Pretty, and gently lowered them onto the branches of the tree outside Freekin's bedroom.

As they crawled in through the window, Pretty's kitties swirled around her, meowing with joy that she was home. She gave them love and then she snapped her fingers at Scary.

"Make microscope," she commanded him.

He settled onto Freekin's desk with a sweet little smile and changed into a microscope.

"Ta da, Freekin!" Pretty said. "We so helping!"

"Wow, incredible!" Freekin cried. "Does it really work?"

Pretty gave him a look as if to say, *Duh*. "Spy plane works. Helicopter works. Microscope works."

"Sweet! Okay, tell me what to do, and I'll help you," Freekin offered. He held out his hand for a down-low. "We're a team!"

"Yes, yes, yes, Freekin," she said happily, slapping his palm with hers. "Team Pretty Freekin Scary! Wheee!"

She zoomed in a circle. Her kitties flew around her in a crazed herd, chasing after her tentacles.

✶ ✶ ✶

"Freekin, hydrogen peroxide," Pretty said, holding out her hand as she peered through the Scary-scope. It was nearly one A.M. Back at his house, Tuberculosis was still asleep. Half a dozen windows were open on Freekin's desktop computer, containing a set of blueprints for the Mystery Meat factory, and articles about *Apatheticus Majoris*. They had located the Ultra Top Secret Enhancement Laboratory, as well as two long tubes with nozzles labeled GLITTERIZATION SPRAYERS. Two large cylindrical shapes labeled TOASTY TWINKLE TANKS were attached to the tubes. That was where they would place the antidote—if they could get it made in time!

Freekin handed Pretty the bottle of peroxide. She dribbled a little bit on the slide and placed it beneath the viewer. Although he was trying hard not to show it, Freekin was beginning to lose hope. Pretty and Scary had done a masterful job of working on an antidote—Scary managed to transform into several chemicals Pretty needed for her research, and Pretty heated up the resulting solutions with flames from her mouth. But they were nearly out of time, and nothing

150

was working. Maybe when Tuberculosis got back up, he would be able to pick up a trail from their many, many failed experiments. But he'd have to do it soon.

Freekin shifted his weight. He wasn't tired, but he was edgy. He wanted to know how Lilly was.

"Maybe we should take a break," Freekin suggested. He picked up his guitar and strummed very softly, not wanting to wake up his parents.

"She's a little monster, yeah," he sang.

Pretty turned her head and glanced at him.

"But she's my little monster, yeah." He grinned at her and tried a box chord progression. He thought for a moment. And then he sang another line.

"Calms me when I'm feelin' fears,
Has tentacles and ponytail ears,
She so Pretty."

"Oooh, Freekin," Pretty cooed. She blew kissies at him.

Giving her a wink, he tried another verse:
"Her spinning eyes can freak you out.
Sometimes she rotates while she shouts.
Mess with my monster, I'll knock you out!
She's a little monster, yeah.
But she's my little monster, yeah.
She so Pretty."

And in that moment, that very special, heart-stopping moment, Pretty could tell she had finally won Freekin's heart. He had *never* sung to Yucky Lilly that way. He had never even *smiled* at Yucky Lilly. Around her, he was tense and unhappy.

Around Pretty, he was winky-blinky and singy-wingy.

Floaty with joy, she peered through the Scary-scope. *Oh, Freekin, he so undead cutie-pie . . . He so . . . so . . .*

Pretty gasped. The viruses were not moving!

"Yee-ha!" she shrieked. "Pretty does it! Pretty does it!" She bounced up and down on her tentacles and jabbed her finger toward the slide. "Freekin! Freekin looks!"

Freekin put down the guitar and rushed up beside her. "Do you think you did it? Really?"

"Freekin looks!" she insisted.

He peered in. There were lots of little *zzzzzzzs*, but none of them were wriggling around, the way they had been all night. "Wow," he said. "Do you think they're dead?"

"They so dead dead dead!" she cried. "Pretty kill viruses! Grrr!" Her eyes spun. Her fangs clacked.

"You little genius! You did it! Oh, Pretty, I love you!" He picked her up and whirled her in a circle.

Freekin love Pretty, she thought, swooning. In all her million-plus years, she had never been so utterly, deliriously happy.

"Pretty love Freekin," she whispered as he set her down on her tentacles. Tears of joy streamed down her face.

"No one knew that a simple mixture of one part hydrogen peroxide to three parts vanilla extract could neutralize Toasty Twinkle, and save Snickering Willows from disaster. I congratulate you and your sister," Tuberculosis said as he disabled the alarm at Snickering Willows Foodatorium. Luckily, the store was two short blocks from Tuberculosis's house.

Freekin and Pretty followed him inside the dark, empty store. Tuberculosis grabbed a shopping cart and shined his flashlight on the rows of canned goods and boxes of pasta. Although Tuberculosis didn't know it, the flashlight Pretty was holding was actually Scary.

"Tuberculosis rush-rush-rush," Pretty begged him, pointing Scary at the clock beneath a sign that read NEAPOLITAN NACHO SOLD OUT! SORRY! It was almost three thirty in the morning.

"Let's see ... rubbing alcohol ... foot deodorant ... hydrogen peroxide." Tuberculosis shined his flashlight

on a row of dark brown plastic bottles. "How much do you think we need?"

"Well, there were about a dozen boxes on the shelf in the hallway. I assume each one held a vial of Toasty Twinkle. We killed our sample with half a cup of peroxide and a tablespoon of vanilla extract," Freekin said. "So if you multiply that by twelve, that's six cups of peroxide and twelve tablespoons of extract. But let's make some extra batches just in case. Better safe than sorry. For all we know, there were more boxes somewhere else."

"Good point," Tuberculosis said. "I'll get several gallons of peroxide."

"We'll go find the vanilla extract," Freekin told him.

"Good idea. I suggest we also take containers to hold our finished antidote. I don't think I have enough at home."

In short order, they had piled their cart with supplies. Tuberculosis had brought the money he'd been saving to buy *The Complete Works of the Highly Depressing Romantic Poets,* and he placed the coins and bills in the cash register along with an anonymous note apologizing for taking the items and assuring that no harm had been intended.

After that, they hurried to Tuberculosis's basement to mix their batch of antidote. By the time they were finished, it was nearly five A.M.!

"Okay, we're leaving for the factory," Freekin informed Tuberculosis as they packed sixteen canning jars sloshing with Toasty Twinkle antidote back into one of the shopping carts.

"I still think I should go with you," Tuberculosis said. "How are you going to get there on time? And you'll need help when you get there."

"I have help," Freekin said, putting his arm around Pretty and giving her a squeeze. Pretty cooed. "Don't worry about us. We have a few tricks up our sleeves."

"Freekin have tricks," Pretty affirmed. "Freekin have lesions."

"You're so funny," Tuberculosis told her with a wink. Pretty blushed and giggled.

Tuberculosis turned to Freekin. "I'll wait to hear from you. I'm not going to school until I do." The goth shuddered. "I don't want to be zombified."

"Me neither," Freekin said. He turned to Pretty. "Let's go. It's time for Operation Anti-Twinkle."

Chapter Twelve:
In Which Our Heroes
Act Heroically!

As soon as Tuberculosis shut his basement door, Pretty and Freekin hopped inside the Scary supersecret spy plane and took off for the Snickering Willows Mystery Meat Factory. Dawn streaked the sky. It was almost 5:15 in the morning. They were cutting it so close!

"Pretty," Freekin began as she piloted the plane over the smokestacks. He looked at her hard. "This could be

very dangerous. You didn't come to the Land of the Living for this. But . . . maybe I did. Maybe this is why I'm really here. I won't be mad if you and Scary back out. If you can just get me there, I'll put the antidote in the glitterization tanks alone."

"Freekin so dum-dum," she said sweetly. "Pretty helps her Freekin! Scary helps!"

"Zibu," the Scary supersecret spy plane said, perhaps with slightly less enthusiasm.

Freekin smiled gratefully at her. "You and Scary are one of a kind."

"Oh," she murmured softly. "Oh, Freekin."

* * * *

Freekin loves his Pretty, Pretty thought joyfully as they landed the plane. Scary transformed into a wheeled packing crate for the bottles of antidote. Using the blueprints, Freekin located the locker room where the yellow hazardous materials suits were stored. He put the top half of one on Pretty—a helmet and a heavy sort of shirt—and climbed into one himself. They looked like astronauts!

"ATTENTION! ONLY TEN MORE MINUTES TO GLITTERIZATION!" a loud, metallic voice announced. "PERSONNEL REPORT TO YOUR DESIGNATED POSTS!"

"We have to hurry," Freekin said through his mask as he folded up the blueprints and stuck them in a pocket of his thick yellow pants. His voice was breathy and electronic.

As they walked out of the locker room, men and women rushed in, grabbing hazmat suits off hooks and climbing into them. Freekin tried to act casually until they got around the corner. Then they raced down a hallway to an elevator marked ULTRA TOP SECRET ENHANCEMENT LABORATORY.

They leaped in and the door shut. But as the elevator lifted upward, someone banged on the door.

"Wait!" a man shouted. "We need to get up there!"

"C'mon, c'mon," Freekin whispered, willing the elevator to move faster.

Finally it opened into a hallway facing a door with a glowing yellow rectangle. They had expected this; Scary changed from the packing crate into a paper-thin shape that slid beneath the door and opened it for Freekin and Pretty.

"ATTENTION! ONLY NINE MORE MINUTES TO GLITTERIZATION!"

On the other side of the door, a narrow, dark corridor was dimly lit by purple bands of neon. As Scary

enclosed himself around the bottles of antidote once more, Freekin took Pretty's hand and together they moved cautiously down the passageway. Soon other people in suits joined them, jostling around Scary and fretting about getting to their assigned spots in time.

"We're almost there," Freekin whispered, giving Pretty a little squeeze. His voice through the mask sounded metallic and foreign. "There should be a flight of stairs right . . . here."

But there wasn't.

"ATTENTION! ONLY EIGHT MORE MINUTES TO GLITTERIZATION!"

"Now what?" Freekin muttered, reaching for the blueprints. The stairs were clearly marked on the document, but they weren't there in real life.

"Let's look farther down," Freekin said. They kept going. The countdown kept progressing.

"ATTENTION! ONLY THREE MORE MINUTES TO GLITTERIZATION!"

"Freekin!" Pretty tugged on his hand. "Looky!"

Just ahead, there was a plain metal door marked STAIRS.

"I don't know if it's the right one," Freekin said. "But I don't know what else to do." He gave a sharp nod. "Let's hustle!"

Scary went underneath and opened it.

Uh-oh.

There was a fellow "astronaut" on the other side. A guard. He was holding what appeared to be some kind of weapon across his chest, and he aimed it straight at Freekin.

"State your business," the guard said.

Freekin cleared his throat in an effort to make it lower.

"We're here for the final inspection," he said.

"*What* final inspection?" the other man demanded.

"ATTENTION! THERE IS ONE MORE MINUTE TILL GLITTERIZATION! SIXTY SECONDS! FIFTY-NINE . . . FIFTY-EIGHT . . . FIFTY-SEVEN . . ."

Suddenly red and white lights began flashing, and a high-pitched WHOOP-WHOOP-WHOOP sound rattled the bones in Freekin's head.

We're not going to make it, Freekin thought. *No! I'd give anything to do this. I'd go back to the Afterlife, or somewhere worse. If only . . . oh, Lilly, I'm sorry. Mom, Dad, Raven, Steve . . .* All the people he cared about flashed through his mind. And then his brain seized on the image of beautiful Lilly, and he knew he must not fail her.

"Freekin," Pretty whispered, "Pretty makes scene."

And what a scene it was! Pretty rushed the man, picked him up, and tossed him into the hall. Then she tossed Freekin into the hall, too. She turned to Scary.

"Scary saves antidote!" she cried, kicking him to safety along with Freekin. She slammed the door shut and gazed down into the bowels of the Ultra Top Secret Enhancement Laboratory. There were no other people there, just the twin tanks, and the tubes, and the nozzles! They were positioned on either side of a conveyer belt, waiting to spray Toasty Twinkle zombie juice on the twelve perfect gray squares of Mystery Meat bobbing along on that very belt.

"INITIATE GLITTERIZATION PROCEDURES!" the electronic voice ordered.

The nozzles spewed glittery gold liquid all over the first square in the line.

"GAZEEKLIELIKKEEEEEZA!" Pretty screamed, resorting to her native language as she leaped commando-style onto the top of the stair rail and tore off her mask and hazmat top.

"KAZEELEELEELILO!" she shrieked at a volume and intensity only a one-million-year-old monster named Pretty could manage. Flames shot from her seven eyeballs and her clacking, fanged mouth. She screamed again,

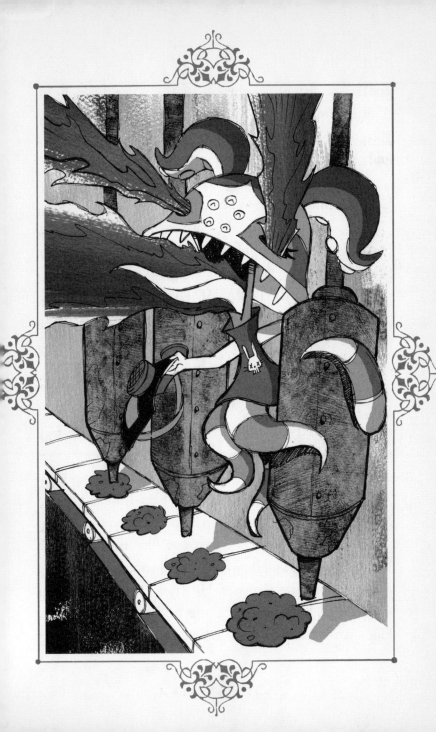

and more flames mushroomed from her little head. A firestorm erupted in a swirl of orange and red. The glitterization material turned white hot! Smoke billowed and churned.

"Pretty!" Freekin shouted behind her. He took her hand. "Come on! Get out of there!"

She shook him off. She was on her Pretty mission. She had to do this for her Freekin! She had to make sure everything was all gone!

"GAZEEELIILALALALALWAZU!" she screamed.

And then the whole place blew sky-high! Pretty shot up into the smoke and fire . . .

And everything went black.

"You're sure she's going to be okay?" Freekin asked as he laid Pretty on the bed in his room. Her little face was smudged with smoke and ashes, but her breath was gentle as she slept.

"*Zibu,*" Scary assured him. He leaned over and gave Pretty six butterfly kisses, and a nosey-nosey, too.

Freekin had searched through the rubble of the Ultra Top Secret Enhancement Laboratory to find the unconscious little monster. He cradled her in his arms and carried her to safety as the lab continued to burn. Floor after floor of the Snickering Willows Mystery

Meat Factory collapsed. Scary flew them away, with one single antidote jar intact.

"Okay. I'm going to take the antidote over to Lilly's." Freekin ran a finger along Pretty's cheek. "What a brave, wonderful little monster," he said.

Scary patted Pretty. Then he waved bye-bye to Freekin, as if assuring him that it was safe to go. So Freekin took the jar and hurried out of the house.

The sky was thick with smoke. The aftermath of the fire was so bad that school had been canceled. Freekin was grateful that he didn't have to breathe the air. And that his eyes weren't stinging. There really was a lot to be said for being undead.

He jogged over to Lilly's house and rapped on her window. When there was no response, he rapped on it again. And a third time.

Dull-eyed and expressionless, Lilly came to the window. She stared at him as if she didn't know who he was.

Freekin pushed open the window. He worried about exposing her to the smoke for too long. "Hey, how are you?" he asked her in a soft voice.

Again, she did not react at all to the fact that he had asked her a question.

"Fine. Just fine," she said.

"Here, I brought you this." He showed her the jar. "I want you to drink just a little."

"Yes, Freekin," she said. Her voice was flat. She parted her lips.

He put the jar to her lips. She drank. Then her eyes began to flutter and—sparkle. The lights were back on.

"Brad?" she said.

"What?" Freekin cried. "No, I'm—"

"There you are!" Brad bellowed as he stomped up to Freekin. He grabbed his shoulder and whirled him along. "I've been looking for you, you freak!" He shook his fist in Freekin's face. "You brainwashed Lilly into liking you again with your powers of the undead!"

"He did not!" Lilly shouted at him. She was herself again! She was de-zombiefied! "I broke up with you because you took me for granted, Brad!"

"And now you're trying to make me jealous with this freak here!" he screamed. Then he took a swing at Freekin. Blinded by his anger, he missed.

———— *—*—*—* ————

"Oh my Freekin," Pretty murmured as she stopped dead on the sidewalk in front of Yucky Lilly's house and stared at the three people shouting and arguing. She heard it all. She saw it all. Especially the glow on Freekin's face, which was practically impossible to miss. "Oh Yucky

Lilly." Her seven bloodshot eyes filled with tears, which streamed down her sooty face. Her lips trembled. Her shoulders sagged.

She had awakened to discover that her Freekin was gone. Scary had told her he had come here to give Lilly the antidote, and she had had a scared feeling in her heart, and in her throat . . . a scared feeling that Freekin didn't love his Pretty after all. Not like he loved Yucky Lilly.

Why Lilly? Why? she thought, as her world shattered. She had done everything she could for Freekin, *everything*. Risked her life to finish what he had started . . . item number four on her list to Get Her Freekin could have read: *Save the world.*

"Bwah!" she cried.

She trundled away as she had the day of his trial, losing track of herself for a moment . . . and then it came to her. What Brad had said about jealousy . . . maybe she could make her Freekin jealous! Make him realize he'd taken his Pretty for granted!

Pretty had the perfect plan. As a monster from the Underworld, she had the ability to summon *other* monsters from the Underworld, too. And not just any ol' monsters. *Boy* monsters! Ha! So she raced as fast as her tentacles would carry her to the graveyard.

She stood at the peak of the tallest hill in the whole yard and took in her surroundings. Ashes fell like snowflakes as she pushed up the sleeves of her smoky jumper and took a deep breath. She seemed to grow about twenty feet tall and twenty feet wide. She was as big as the crushing machine at the factory! Her eyes spun and smoke rose from the top of her head. Fire blasted out of her mouth as she threw back her head and yelled at the top of her lungs:

"GOOGALBALALILIWAZU!"

It began to snow for real.

She tried again, raising her arms skyward:

"GOOGALBALALILIWAZU!"

On the third try, she imagined the most handsome, most tentacled, most eyeballed, toothiest boy monster in all the land.

"GOOGALBALALILIWAZU!"

The earth shook. Pretty lost her balance and pitched forward, rolling into a ball, gathering snow as she caromed against a headstone. She hit it with a thunk.

The writing on the headstone read:

SWEENY BURTON

R.I.P.

BELOVED FRIEND

DATE OF DEATH

AUGUST 31ST

"Bad ingredients!" she shrieked, remembering the skull in the box at the factory. SB AUG 31. "Oh no!"

She was rushing off to tell Freekin what she had just figured out when the earth shook again. Then the air shimmered, coalescing into a shadow, and then into a shape. And then the shape . . . became a man. Not a monster man, but a human man. Or . . . a former human man.

Even though the man was covered with sores and lesions, and most of him was white skeleton bone, Pretty recognized him right away. In his coat, vest, and baggy pants, there was no mistaking him from the statue beside the fountain in the park and the painting of him in the library.

"You so Snickering III!" Pretty screamed, pointing at him.

"Yes, Miss Pretty, it is I," the man said. "Horatio Snickering III, the founder of Snickering Willows, the creator of Mystery Meat, and the man who decreed there should be no questions. I hope you don't mind, but I took advantage of your summoning spell to return to the Land of the Living. I see that things have gone terribly awry in my town."

She wasn't sure she knew what awry meant. "Bad Men?" she asked, to see if she was getting his point. She

hoped he wasn't too angry about his factory. Maybe he didn't know about it.

"Yes, bad men," he agreed. His smile was very kind, even though he didn't have any lips left.

"Certain . . . people have disrupted the order I created. It is so unfortunate." He cocked his head. "I understand that you and your friend Freekin just saved the town from a terrible virus."

"Freekin," she choked, drooping. In all the excitement, she had almost forgotten about her broken heart. "Freekin so hero."

"Yes, my dear, but *you* so Pretty." He smiled again. "My heroic little friend. Pretty, I want to make things right for Snickering Willows. I want to rid my town once and for all of undesirable elements. You can help me."

"Pretty helps?" she asked, blinking her tear-swollen eyes at him.

"Yes, Pretty helps." He leaned forward. "But here's the thing. You've seen how dangerous this sort of thing can be. I think he'd be better off if he wasn't involved. He might get hurt."

"You so true," she said. What if Freekin had burned up in the fire? She wasn't certain what would have happened to him then.

"But you two are so close," Horatio Snickering III pondered aloud.

Pretty pondered along with him. "Secret?" she suggested.

He frowned slightly. A maggot crawled along his eyebrow, reminding her of the squares of Mystery Meat riding the conveyer belt.

"I don't know. He's so heroic. And so . . . inquisitive. I think it would be better if there were simply no chance at all that he could interfere. I mean, participate."

She considered that.

"Did you know that you, and you alone, are able to put people to sleep simply by frightening them a little? It's called a terror-induced coma. That's what you did to Dr. Lao and Ed Wood. You almost did it to Freekin the other night, too."

"Pretty can?" She had never known that. She wasn't surprised. She was a very clever and powerful little monster.

"Yes. You can do that." He snapped the finger bones of his left hand together. "Here's an idea! Maybe you could put Freekin into a coma like that . . . for his own good . . . watch the watch, Pretty, watch the watch, you're getting sleepy . . ."

She blinked. While the man was talking, he pulled something shiny out of his half-rotted vest pocket with the finger bones of his right hand. It was a watch, on a gold chain. He swung it back and forth, back and forth . . . her eyes blinked again. Her lids grew heavy.

"That's right, Pretty, listen to my voice . . . do as I say . . ."

"Yes, Horatio Snickering III . . ." Pretty said drowsily. She so hypnotized . . .

＊ ＊ ＊ ＊

"Alone at last," Lilly sighed as she climbed out of her window. Now that the Snickering Willows Municipal Fire Department had put out the enormous fire at the Mystery Meat factory, the sky was beginning to clear of smoke. Brad had cleared off, too, promising revenge, telling Freekin to watch his back . . . and his head . . . and all the bones in his body.

Then Raven had come by, asking Freekin for the antidote. Tuberculosis had given him a smidge of Toasty Twinkle to help Shadesse get over CSS faster, and now she needed the counteracting elixir.

"Yes, alone at last," Freekin said.

It was getting dark. The long day was ending. As the moon rose over Snickering Willows, Freekin laced his fingers with Lilly's.

"So, you really broke up with Brad," he said.

She smiled sweetly at him and nodded. "I really did."

Ask her, he ordered himself. *Ask her now. Don't be stupid.*

"So . . . would you . . ." he began. Then he stopped.

She lifted a brow.

"Sorry, question," he said. "Once you start asking questions, it's hard to stop."

"It's all right," Lilly murmured, blinking at him with her big blue eyes. "I like it when you ask me questions." She tilted her head at him as they walked along the street where she lived.

"Okay." He took a breath. *Would you kiss me?*

That was what he planned to ask. It truly was. It would solve everything. It would guarantee that he wouldn't have to return to the Afterlife . . . or worse. It would mean that Lilly was his one true love. But all he could muster the courage for was this:

"Would you like to go to the Nonspecific Winter Holiday Dance with me?" Which was also a good question. A great question, in fact. Lilly was positively elated.

"Oh, yes, Freekin," she replied, beaming at him with her beautiful, very blue eyes. "Very, very much."

And the two strolled on.

This is Belle. I am begging you not to draw this one out. I can't stand it anymore. Did he kiss her? Yes or no? Do they live happily ever after or is he sent back to the Afterlife?

Oh, my dear Belle. My sweet, young, innocent, dear Belle. I wish I could help you. I really do. But as any of my Gentle Readers will tell you—it's a little more complicated than that. I wouldn't be doing my job if I just gave you a simple, straightforward answer. And as a past and hopefully future member of the International Order of Narrators, I take my job very seriously. So for now I'll leave you and all my Gentle Readers on this note—with Freekin and his beloved Lilly enjoying their romantic stroll in the rather heavily polluted air, unaware of the devious plans of Horatio Snickering III and his unsuspecting accomplice—and we shall say that in that moment, they were very, very happy.